My Sister and I

(A novel by Sean-Paul Thomas)

Hope you enjoy the Book Miriam

Chapter 1

My earliest memory of my father's violence was when I was around five years old. I remember sitting in the back seat of our old beat up five-door ford escort. It was cold and dark outside as we travelled along a lonely highland road where the only faded light came from a full but faintly clouded moon that had just slunk down behind one of the dark and brooding mountain tops that hovered over us like some gigantic sleeping dinosaur.

We might have been driving back from the local town, or even Glasgow perhaps—which was around a four-hour drive south from our farm house in one of the remotest regions of the Scottish Highlands, or we could've just been out and about for a wee random winter drive in amongst the beautiful snow swept highland valleys and mountains. I can't quite be sure. Although, my father did enjoy his random, spur of the moment drives and ventures out into the wilderness, so it could have been that more than anything else.

Mother wasn't there, I recall that much. Just Dad, sitting up front by himself, singing along to his Bruce Springsteen greatest hit tunes on the car stereo while my twin sister and I sat silently in the back with our seatbelts firmly fastened.

In fact, if I recall correctly, my sister was sleeping soundly in the back beside me, although she could have just as easily been in one of her foul, demonic moods and refusing to speak to me for some reason or another.

That night it seemed like we were the only other people out there on that isolated highland road. Everywhere around us seemed so calm and peaceful as my father continued to drive along in good spirits, safely sticking to the fifty miles per hour speed limit like he always did, while singing with his heart and soul to some imaginary concert audience sitting behind the windscreen, out in the road in front of him. An audience that only he could see.

I remember feeling him tense up all of a sudden. Only a little at first as his singing became less frequent and passionate until he ceased from singing out altogether. Concert over for the time being.

He kept anxiously glancing into his rear-view mirror, every so often at first, then it seemed that he spent more and more time gazing into it than he did paying attention to the road up ahead. The next thing I knew a pair of bright headlights from behind us were swiftly shining in through the rear.

Another vehicle was fast upon us. A larger one than ours, possibly a van or a big jeep. It had sped up on us over the past few miles, going well over the national speed limit, and now sat impatiently tailgating our smaller car from behind.

So, this was what had caused my father's new anxious state of mind. He hated anyone speeding up behind him, especially too fast and reckless, when there was clearly no need for such bullish behaviour and on a quiet country road too, with all that beautiful stunning scenery every which way one looked.

"Why is every cunt aw-ways in such a fuckin' rush these days, eh?" he always used to say while shaking his head in absolute disgust when other cars and lorries drove right up behind him, like he wasn't even there. "Why would ye no just wantae go as slow as you can drivin doon these magnificent roads, or even stop and pull over for a wee minute, get the hell oot yur damn fuckin car and just take in aw this bloody great gorgeousness and fresh clean air. Ah dinnae ken." He finished with a deep sigh and another shake of his head.

Observing him over the years, he usually—nine times out of ten—just pulled over into the next available parking or passing bay and let the impatient driver or drivers pass him by with only a dirty scowl on his face and a shame-on-you glint in his eye as they sped on by, continuing on their merry way. But something was different this time. Something was dangerously off inside my father's head that night. A switch had been well and truly flipped and I was seeing it for the very first time.

The driver of the van sitting tucked up, bumper to bumper directly behind us, had begun to push all my father's very few trigger buttons all at the same time.

First button: he was tailing so dangerously close to our car on such a treacherous highland road, obnoxiously disrespecting the national speed limit and failing to keep a safe distance from the vehicle in front, which was two seconds, he'd always say, in dry conditions, and six seconds in icy wet conditions, such as it was in this very situation.

Second button: the driver behind us was flashing his headlights over and over again, like his car was having some kind epileptic seizure, before leaving them on full beam, temporarily blinding everyone inside our car. Putting the lives of not just my father in danger, but the lives of his two-innocent-wee-darling-daughters seated in the back.

And third: the ignorant, arrogant driver was now tooting his horn for my dad to pull over or just move the hell aside and let him pass.

The only problem with that plan of action was that there happened to be no good passing points that my father could see in the darkness up ahead for him to pull over and into. He needed some time to find a good safe spot and this 'arsehole, baw-jawed bastard, cunt bag' —father's words—just wasn't allowing him the time to do that.

I was beginning to see an insane and uncontrollable rage brewing in my father's eyes, slowly but surely taking over his recent placid energy. At the time, it terrified the life out of me because it was the first time I'd ever seen him morphing into such an enraged, demonic creature. Although, it was by no means to be the last that I ever witnessed such an act. It's just that the first time is always the most shocking. It's the one that sticks with you the most, and so much more than all the others that came thick and fast over the next few years. It's the first memory you always carry with you, even when you see it happening all over again and again, in even greater, gorier detail.

What happened next though transpired so fast. Like a snap of someone else's fingers right in front of my face. Anger and hate engulfed him. It raged through every ounce of fibre in his being like some out of control freight train.

Then it happened.

Without any warning to the driver behind, or any consideration for his daughters' safety tucked up in the back seat, dad braked violently hard.

My sister, who had been sleeping soundly up until that point, suddenly found herself jolted awake. We stared at each other in absolute dread as the large van ploughed hard into the back of our car with the most deafening crash and bang of crushed metal on metal. Within seconds we came to a shuddering halt in the middle of the deserted road, as did the van with its front bonnet crushed up into the back of us. Without any hesitation, my father swiftly blazed from the car like some freak force of nature. He seemed completely oblivious that my sister and I were even there at all and might even be hurt from the collision. And without checking to see if we were all right, he yanked out a hidden baseball bat, from behind the front driver's seat.

Immediately, I unclicked my seatbelt. My sister did the same before we both clambered swiftly onto our knees and up onto the back seats of the car. With curious eyes, still caught in a frozen, dream-like aura of shock, horror, and excitement, we watched as my father approached the van and dragged a bearded and dazed, stocky older gentleman out from the driver's seat of the smashed-up vehicle. Then without a single thought for mercy, regret or consequences, our father began to beat and pound the holy living hell out of the man, with stroke after brutal stroke from the full length of his bat—to the man's chest, arms, legs, and head.

When the man became motionless and no longer seemed to be putting up any kind of fight or resistance— when all life appeared to be pummelled from every ounce of his body and soul, well that was when my father proceeded to use the soles of his big, black, leather, steel-toe-capped boots to stamp and crush the poor man's head to a total bloody pulp on the tarmac.

I remember compelling myself to hurriedly turn away at that point and hide my face in my hands as the brutal, vicious acts of horror became far too much for my young innocent eyes to handle and my small child brain to comprehend.

My sister, on the other hand, continued to watch the severe act of violence without any feeling whatsoever. At first her face looked expressionless like she was watching some late-night adult TV show that she wasn't really supposed to be watching but couldn't care less if someone happened to walk in and catch her anyway. Like she'd seen it all before. If it wasn't for the tiniest flicker of a faded grin upon her angelic face then I would have just figured that perhaps she had no emotion about the situation at all, good or bad. But secretly, I knew in that moment she was loving my father's brutal actions and learning from it too. Soaking in all that fiery rage and terrible violence into her not so innocent sponge like brain.

When the sick thudding noises of boot upon crushed bone and flesh came to an abrupt halt, I gradually found the courage to glance back up and out of the window again. My father had finally exhausted his efforts to pound the man's head and body into the ground. He then dragged the dead man—who I sincerely hoped was dead or else I couldn't imagine the pain and suffering he'd be going through—back up onto his feet before bundling him into his van again but on the passenger side.

Dad then climbed into the driver's compartment and reversed the vehicle away from our own car before accelerating forward and pulling up alongside us. He climbed out of the van and approached us. He then leaned into the driver's side door and gave us both a warm, reassuring smile. So, he had remembered that we were there after all.

"Ye's baeth awright, aye?"

We both nodded in unison but said nothing more. Words were not needed in that moment only our calm, cold expressions that told him that we were both fine and unphased with everything that had just gone down.

"That's ma girls. Strong as fuckin Rhinos, eh? just like their fuckin da."

He gave us a firm, cocky wink that said everything was going to be fine because he was back in charge of the situation. He told us to stay in the car and not get out or go for a bloody wander while he was away. He said that he wouldn't be long. He said he had to drop his friend off somewhere safe and sound and that he'd be back real soon to take us home.

I think we waited for around thirty minutes or so. Only one other car passed us by on the lonely highland road during that time, but lucky for them, they didn't stop. My sister and I kept our heads down low when it drove past, just like Dad had taught us to do when he wasn't around. He wasn't a big fan of nosy strangers either.

I was about to fall asleep in my sister's lap when the loud, violent sound of the driver's side door swinging open then shut again jolted me awake. My out-of-breath father had thrown himself back inside our car.

"Fuckin freezin oot there the night girls, eh? Jeezo."

My father didn't wait for an answer. He'd already started the engine and was soon driving off, back along the dark and lonely highland road. His car back to being the only other vehicle out on the road once again, just the way he liked it.

Without words, my sister and I resumed our seated positions in the backseat and clicked our seat belts back into place. On went the CD player again and, just like nothing had ever happened, our dad began singing once more—full swing, full passion. Normality resumed.

A few minutes later I remember gazing out of the car window as an old stone bridge emerged from the darkness in front of us. A rip-roaring river wound its way down from a higher valley to flow right underneath the bridge. On the right side of the bridge, half of the old stone barrier had come away from the edge like something big and heavy—perhaps the size of another car like ours—had smashed right through it.

Sure enough, as we slowed down to cross the single file bridge, I could just about make out the dark outline of the van from earlier. Its front end totally submerged in the freezing cold-water depths of the murky riverbed below while it's rear-end poked straight out of the rough flowing, ice cold water, shiny and glistening in the moonlight.

As we drove across the bridge, my father stopped singing for a moment. He grinned then snorted out hard.

"Ooof. Looks like a sore one that, eh? Bad luck fella. Al need tae report that tae the station first thing in the morn."

And with that my father began singing out to the high heavens once again.

Chapter 2

I'm now almost thirteen years old and I hate my father more than anything else in the world. In fact, I have more hate for him in this very moment than I ever did at any other previous point in our troubled and turbulent history together.

Everyone who used to know us in the local area and saw us around the community, whether that be at our school or around the neighbouring town almost fifteen miles away, now believe— thanks to our father—that we have gone off to live with our Mother, a mother we've never officially known or even met, back down in Glasgow.

The truth of the matter is that our mother has been missing from our lives for longer than we've had memories. And recently our father even pulled us out of the local village school when one of the new teachers started asking too many questions regarding our mysterious upbringing, along with questions about the source of the constant marks and bruises no twelve-year-old girls should ever have on their bodies. Bruises and marks that our father didn't physically put there himself, but nonetheless is still one hundred percent a contributor of.

You see, our father grew up in the wilderness—the glorious Scottish highland lochs, valleys, forests, and mountains that you see every which way you look in this neck of the woods. His own father, who my sister and I never had the pleasure of meeting— thank god—is always mentioned by our father like he was some kind of ancient, magnificent god of men. He made our father grow up in the wild too, living, working, hunting, and surviving in the great outdoors and now our father does exactly the same thing to his own children. A passing down of his family values, ideals, and traditions, no less.

When our father was a wee boy, our granddad told, preached, and convinced him—although I say *brainwashed*—that something truly awful was going to happen to the world and mankind, someday very soon, and that only the ones who prepared for it and put in the brutal effort and hard work to ready themselves for the imminent, world-wide disaster to come would be the ones who would truly survive this ever-nearing, brutal apocalypse, and thus eventually emerge from the death and destruction to drive mankind onwards into a new era. A better era. A better world and place. A better place where the world could take all the time it needed to recover from the sins, destruction and devastation that mankind had inflicted upon it.

Ever since my sister and I were old enough to walk, our father had passed this knowledge and ideas, along with his family traditions and philosophies, down onto us—his only two daughters and blood kin still alive – or that I know of.

Every day, for as long as I can remember, he has drilled and trained the mantra *survival-of-the-fittest* into us like it was the only thing that mattered in our screwed-up existence. And to him, it really was *the only thing* that ever did matter in our screwed-up way of live.

From the age of six onwards our father taught us how to grow vegetables in the dirt, how to source water from the ground when there was no sign of any rivers or water for miles around. He taught us how to set traps and snares to catch small wild animals and fish, how to gut them, skin them, and cook those same animals, how to build a camp with branches and wood and put a roof over our heads in the heart of a storm while in the middle of nowhere. He taught us how to make dangerous weapons from the earth's natural resources so that we could hunt and kill larger animals like dogs, deer, stray goats, cows, horses, and yes, even people sometimes too, for when the time came. Which it eventually did, but much sooner than I thought it might. But I'll come to that later.

He taught us how to make fire by using two pieces of dried wood and a little bit of kindle (dry grass or an old bird's nest). But most important of all, he taught us how to look after ourselves. How to survive in the world when we had nothing on our person but our own two hands to assist us.

My sister was always the one though that showed more of a keen and eager interest in these torturous survival skills and monthly exercise drills that our father constantly put us through.

She adored them so much and learned so quickly and skilfully, even finding ways to apply them into her everyday life, that she always looked forward to father's next lessons, tasks, and adventures more than anything else in her life.

To put it into context, she was the perfect student for him and he was the ideal teacher for her. Father psychopath and daughter psychopath, side by side.

For the first few years and up until the age of ten, my father enjoyed nothing more than taking his girls way out into the remotest regions of the Scottish wilderness for days, sometimes weeks on end, and camping out from scratch. We'd leave the old family farm house, which was passed down to him by his own father, at first light and make our way hiking across the mountains and valleys, always in a different direction each time, with no food, no water, no rucksacks, or camping equipment to our names. Just the wind, rain, and rare Scottish sunshine on our backs.

It was a challenge from him to see how long we could survive out there in the bare-knuckled wild. How long we could keep it together inside, mentally and physically, until he decided that we'd had enough or until one of us became badly ill or severely dehydrated or poisoned by some random inedible berry or mushroom or uncooked piece of squirrel which, nine times out of ten, was usually, always me.

That first hour or so of starting out from the house, with nothing in your hands and only the cold Scottish sun on your back, and that intense pressure and excitement to find some water, make a fire, catch and cook some food, and to find and make a new shelter out of branches and leaves or anything you could find before the sun went down. That was always his favourite part— my sister's too— That first part of the adventure when you truly thought that you might die out there unless you got your *bloody arse in gear* (my father's words again).

From a very young age, I always knew that this life was not for me. And I would just have to bide my time until either my father died—hopefully soon, tragically and painfully—perhaps while off on one of his into-the wild expeditions, or, I become an adult, by law, and could finally go off on my own and do what I wanted to do with my life without his demanding sergeant major voice and presence echoing into my ears twenty-four hours a day. Which is funny, since he did use to be a sergeant in the British army for a number of years, or so he told us once, before my sister and I came along and well before he ever met our mysterious mother, who he very rarely ever mentioned or talked about.

The best explanation I ever got out of him one time before he smacked me senseless was that she left us a very long time ago, almost immediately after we were born, to return to her native home of Glasgow. Full stop - *Now, no mare silly fuckin questions* (his words)

It wasn't until our eleventh birthday that my father first made us go survival camping all by ourselves and without the aid and assistance of his presence, skills and knowledge. He'd led us up to the vast mountain forest himself. The one that sat a few miles along the coast from our farm house. But that was as far as his adult supervision was willing to take us on that first occasion.

"M'ber what ah taught ye's, aye?" he'd say while mostly making eye contact with my sister throughout his entire speech. "Yul stay in that forest there for three days and three nights and then al come back and get ye's, right here, right oan this very fuckin spot. Oan the dawn of the fourth day. Dae ye's understand me girls, aye?"

"Yes, sir," my sister eagerly replied, drowning out my own meek answer of acknowledgement.

"The idea is tae survive oot here, girls," he continued. "For as lang as ye's can. And just like ma auld man used tae tell me. Survival of the fittest is what this world will come tae soon enough when the shite finally hits the fan. So, go intae they woods. Make your fire. Make your shelter. Find your water and hunt your food tae feed your wee empty bellies. Live well and be free oot there. Ye's got that? Just like ah taught ye's."

I remember his eyes finally turning to meet mine for the first time that day right after he'd made that little speech.

"Just like ah taught baeth of ye's. Now, fuck off oot ma sight and get tae it. Chop chop."

In silence, my sister and I turned from Dad and casually made our way into the huge, daunting, and unwelcoming woods, lying in wait of our presence. We were children about to embark upon a world that most westernised adults, in this day and age, barely even understood yet alone could survive more than a few hours in.

I always wondered what my father would do or say, or how he would react if anything seriously bad ever did happen to either me or my sister while out on these survival adventures. If one of us got badly hurt or, heaven forbid, died a gruesome, grisly death amidst the trees or the unforgiving mountain top terrains.

I really don't think he'd be that bothered at all, to tell you the truth. He'd most likely just shrug it off more than anything else. Give some stupid explanation that we had lived more than most people in the west do in ten lifetimes and died a good death too while we were at it, and of course, we'd died free. Which was the most important thing of all in his book.

Deep inside I knew that he was absolutely fucking insane. But what could I do? I was an eleven-year-old girl and he was my father. He was my world. He was my pain, my torture, my teacher, my tormentor. He was the only thing that I knew.

"And remember this in-aw, girls," he shouted after us as we approached the first row of dark trees on the edge of the woods. "Al be watching, ye's. Yul no ken when or fae where. But al be aroond watching ye's. So dae me proud in there girls. Dae me fuckin' proud."

In silence we continued to walk into the thick dark forest as my father's words fell from my ears like water off a duck's back.

Chapter 3

For twin sisters we didn't particularly like to talk much—well, to each other for that matter. But that didn't mean we weren't close. Far from it. I would do absolutely anything for my sister and she for me if the circumstance ever arose—and it did on a few occasions. But it just seemed like the only thing about our crazy situation that we could talk about—really talk deeply about—was our father, and I knew that none of us really wanted to ever go there.

Perhaps if our feelings were mutual regarding our father, tormentor, and protector then yes, it might just be a bearable place to venture and plan some kind of escape from his abuse. And let's get this straight: Even though it was never sexual it was child abuse. But because I knew for certain that my sister loved and respected my father so much more than I could ever allow myself to do, then him and his extremist ways were always going to be like treading on thin ice as far as she was concerned.

For most of that morning, on the first day of our venture into the forest, we scoured the entire place for an ideal camping spot to base ourselves upon. After over an hour of searching my sister found the most perfect site, just like she always did, since I was only too happy to just let her get on with it, letting her take charge of the situation and bark her orders.

If I'd happened to be in those woods all by myself then I'd be more than happy to just crawl into the nearest dark, damp hole in the ground or hollowed out tree I could find, eating nothing but the small, edible fruits, plants, and insects in my vicinity while making a lovely wee warm fire for myself to get me through the long, cold, dark nights. That was all I really needed in those situations to see me through, until my father came a calling to take me back home again.

My sister hated sitting around though. She absolutely loathed and detested it and always had to be doing something, or checking up on something, or making that something just a little bigger, better, stronger. She could never sit still for a moment while I could quite happily sit quietly and meekly for hours gradually blending into the mundane background, even fantasying from time to time about one day disappearing into it for good.

My sister told me to go and find anything that we could collect water in then get onto finding enough wood to start a fire with, while she swiftly went to work on making a shelter for us to live in out of branches, sticks and logs. When she was done with that task, she went about setting up her snare traps in and around any animal holes in the ground she could find using some old string and wire she'd found lying around while making the shelter.

She never used to be too bothered about catching animals on the first day of these expeditions. Her priority was always setting up camp first before sourcing water and getting a fire started. She always enjoyed having the second and third day open to go out and hunt, after we'd made our base. In fact, dare I say it, this was her second favourite part of the survival adventure after setting off into the unknown. She loved a good hunt and kill. Savoured it so much that it became almost like an obsession to her over the years. I could sense it in her bones and entire demeanour like some faint and foul rotten odour in the air that followed her around day after day and she couldn't do a damn thing to get rid of it and so it just became a part of her. She loved the thrill of the kill even more than our own father did, and that took some doing. It also scared the hell out of me an awful lot too.

I should have known at that point which direction my sister's future was heading, but we were still kids at the end of the day and I always just assumed that we'd both grow out of it in the near future, or that our father would finally get bored of it all and let us be children for once in our miserable lives, even though we were teenagers now, and finally enjoy a normal and stable upbringing. Go out and have other teenage friends with teenage dreams and adventures. And all of our own making too and not forced upon us by his strict hand and one-sided views and opinions on the world.

Sadly though, that day never came.

My sister finally finished building our sturdy and well-hidden wee shelter and by the evening I had our fire lit and roaring fiercely beside it, all by using two dry sticks and rubbing them furiously together for just over an hour with my wee turf of dry kindle, waiting to catch the sparks just like father had taught me to do. And we had this all achieved well before sunset too.

That was one good thing about living in Scotland in the summer. The weather might be miserable as hell and unpredictable to say the least, but those long summer days and nights, when the sun never set until way after ten o'clock at night, were absolute bliss during our camping expeditions. And as you can no doubt tell, I wasn't a big fan of the dark.

For our water situation, we hadn't managed to find any nearby streams or lochs, although we did know of one huge loch a few miles north of our camp base that we'd visited often with our father, but that could wait until morning.

I'd found some plastic bags along with some plastic bottles scattered around the woods, most likely dumped by campers in the area who couldn't be bothered to carry their crap home with them. The plastic bags, I'd tied to some thick tree branches around our shelter using our shoe laces and other bits of string and wire I'd found to secure them. In time, the dew from the leaves dripped into the bags and into some of the bottles that I'd shoved into a few of the thinner tree branches.

Later that night my sister went out to check up on her traps. Traps that she usually left until morning, but because we'd done such a quick and grand job of building up our camp site, she wanted to give us both a wee reward for all our hard work.

She returned to camp twenty minutes later looking absolutely chuffed to bits. In one hand she carried a bird's nest filled with four, un-hatched, eggs, and in her other hand, swinging by its limp tale, was a fully grown, adult rabbit.

When she placed the rabbit down beside the fire I noticed that the poor wee creature seemed to be whimpering and limping, still barely alive. My sister, of course, knew this ever since she'd released it from its snare trap. But instead of wringing or breaking the poor creature's neck and putting it out of its damn misery like any normal human being would, she instead broke its little legs and paws so that even if she dropped it accidentally or put it down on the ground it wouldn't be able to dash off anywhere in a hurry.

I remembered feeling quite angry at her for that. Being forced to witness another animals' torture and suffering. I watched in utter disgust as my sister then sat down beside me and let the poor rabbit crawl around in agonizing circles, going absolutely nowhere, just round and round in great distress, beside the fire.

Soon, she cracked open two of the eggs from the bird's nest and swallowed the contents raw. She offered me the other two and without words I took the welcomed food offering and swiftly gulped them down.

All eyes then turned to the poor suffering wee rabbit. My sister laid down on her belly and supported her chin with her hands. She took great delight in just watching the bunny as it desperately tried to limp, crawl, and hop away while struggling to keep itself in a straight line.

When she started petting the bloody thing, before swiping it up off the ground to hug and hold in her arms like a warm cuddly toy, that was the final straw for me. I jumped to my feet, enraged, and grabbed the rabbit from her grasp. Before she had time to clamber to her feet and wrestle the creature back, I'd already swung its head hard against the nearest tree, bashing its skull to smithereens and putting it well and truly out of its misery.

My sister frowned, placed her hands down upon her hips, and let out a frustrated sigh. With a bitter disgust she spat onto the raging fire before stomping towards me. She ripped the dead rabbit out of my hands and threw it to the dirt beside the shelter. She took out her small pen knife and dropped to her knees right next to the dead animal. Without even pausing for breath or hesitating to see where the best place would be to start cutting it up, she slit the rabbit's furry skin from head to tail, revealing a bright red streak of flesh before proceeding to gut the thing from the inside out like she'd done it a thousand times before.

An hour later we were both sharing our first meal out in the wild together. A slow roasted rabbit with a side salad of dandelions. For after dinner drinks we drained the mouthfuls of water that had accumulated inside the plastic bags and bottles attached to the trees throughout the day.

The next morning, we went for a long wander east through the forest. When we finally came out onto the other side we were pleasantly surprised to find a small hidden loch, one that we hadn't even known had existed before even though we'd grown up and lived in this secluded area our entire lives.

The loch was quiet and beautiful and would be a good source of water and food for us in the days still to come. The only problem was we weren't alone. On our right hand-side and halfway along the upper sandy beach on the eastern shore, if we squinted our eyes just about right, we could make out a single green tent.

My sister felt enraged and immediately wanted to investigate so we cautiously approached the lonely looking campsite, sticking to the edge of the forest and well undercover as we circled the perimeter of the loch shore. When we reached directly opposite the tent we left the cover of the forest and crawled through the long wild grass, moving as closely to it as we possibly could without being seen or heard.

I thought that it might be the wind at first but it didn't seem strong enough. Something was clearly moving from within the tent, gently causing random ripples down both sides, before suddenly becoming more violent. And then in no time at all, the whole tent began bobbing from side to side with more repetitive movements. We even began to hear the faintest sounds of grunts and groans, too, but none of us could put our finger on what might be happening inside that could cause such a scene. Perhaps, someone struggling to put their tent up in the correct way from the inside out, I hazarded a quick guess. My sister thought that a random bear had trapped itself inside and was now eating its way through the unlucky camper, but I didn't think that we still had bears roaming throughout the Scottish countryside. In school, our history teacher Mr Brown had told us that the last bears and wolves had died out centuries ago in Scotland. But my sister was adamant that one or two still secretly patrolled and inhabited the more remote parts of the Highlands.

Suddenly our questions were answered all at once as two heads burst their way through the half-zipped doorway. Their faces looked red and exhausted, but still they grunted and groaned, like they were wrestling furiously with each other just to see which one of them would get to stay on top of the other.

My sister and I just stared at each other in shock yet slightly bemused. We didn't know which way to look or what to indeed make of the whole bizarre scene. Two heads then swiftly turned into two naked upper bodies, slowly forcing their way out of the tent as they thrust, grunted, and groaned, louder and wilder, yet without a care in the world for anyone or anything outside that might be watching them.

I thought it was a man and a woman at first, but then my sister spat in disgust when she saw that both the naked bodies had boobs. By then I was totally confused myself as to what the hell was happening over there in that tent. Soon, the grunts, cries, and howling moans of ecstasy climaxed into one final thrust of both hips and the two naked adult women collapsed in a joyful heap right into each other's arms.

We continued watching the women in a curious silence as they chatted and whispered sweetly to each other. We were too far away to understand anything they were saying and when they finally pried themselves apart they stood up onto their feet, right outside their tent, naked and exposed for all the world to see yet didn't seem to care one single jot.

I secretly liked and admired their bravado already.

My sister, on the other hand, was right at that very moment, plotting a way to banish them from our turf and out of our lives for good.

We waited a wee while longer until both women wandered on down to the loch's shore to clean themselves up after their sweaty wrestling antics. They seemed to be in good spirits as they waded into the cool, clear calm waters, hand in hand. I watched in fascination as they cleaned each other and splashed water on one another like it was the most natural thing in the whole wide world. They kissed passionately too, every now and again, before going off for a swim around the peaceful loch.

When they appeared to be a good, safe distance away and it looked as if it might take them a good few minutes to swim back, we snuck down towards their tent. My sister instructed me to gather up as much of their inexpensive supplies and belongings as I could possibly carry, from bags of nuts, crisps, bread and peanut butter, even a bottle of vodka. We found a lighter, too, along with a pack of cigarettes. We never touched their mobile phones or wallets though.

By the time the two women had stopped gallivanting around in the water and finally noticed the black smoke and fumes pouring out from their tent, it was too late for them to do anything about it. My sister and I had long since disappeared, of course, just like the two women's up-in-smoke tent and remaining belongings.

Back at our own camp, we dropped off everything that we'd taken from the two women, minus the snacking of a whole jar of peanut butter along the way. When we ventured back out to the Loch an hour later, the strange naked women had packed up whatever had remained from their burnt down campsite, which I can't imagine could have been very much, and fled. Did they even manage to salvage any clothes? I couldn't help but guiltily think. All that remained was a light smoke and the smouldering ashes of their humble campsite. I felt a little bad for them. They had voluntarily embarked into the great outdoors to enjoy themselves and have some fun and peaceful times alone underneath the stars, until my sister and I had mischievously come along and destroyed their relaxing habitat like a sledge hammer to a baby deer's head.

My sister though jumped for sheer joy and high fived me half a dozen times, which I played along with just to keep on her good side. We were all alone again and now had our very own mile wide swimming pool to run amok in. Immediately we stripped off our clothes faster than you could say hallelujah and raced down to the water's edge. We dived straight into the cold fresh water and screamed out with an exhilarated joy when we rose up again.

For a good hour we swam, drank, wrestled (proper wrestled, not like the two strange groaning women), and dived around the crystal-clear loch like there was no tomorrow and we were the only other two people left in the world, and not even our father, who I'm sure was watching somewhere, could ruin the moment.

Well, at least that was my fantasy.

We even talked about moving our own camp a wee bit closer to the loch. But my sister ruled against it in the end. She said we would be more exposed by the water, especially if any more stranger camping folk or families decided to hike or camp nearby, which was, of course, when all the annoying questions would start: *How old are you girls? What are you girls doing out here all by yourselves? Where are your parents? Come with us while we phone the police!*

Father always told us to just turn and run like the wind if we ever encountered such inquiries while out and about on our own, but only if we didn't know the people asking the questions. "Run for the nearest trees, then make your ways fuckin' home," he'd always said.

When we'd finished playing around in the loch, we laid ourselves down upon a secluded part of the shore, hidden away from any prying eyes by the long bushy grass all around us. For about an hour we let the sun dry and tan our skins. When we were mostly dry again, all except for our long jet-black hair, we headed back to our base and munched up the rest of the food that we'd 'acquired' from the women, which wasn't a great deal to be honest, just a lot of dried cereal, some fruit, packets of nuts, and crisps. We downed it all in no time. Well, all except for those cigarettes and alcohol.

We vowed to return to the loch a few hours before sunset and try to catch some fish for dinner using the plastic bottles we'd gathered from around the woods. We could make wee bottle traps to catch smaller fish in or even make a small fishing line with our boot laces and left-over string from my sister's snare traps. We'd found some old coat hangers too, so we could make a hook to tie to the end with some insects speared onto it as bait. Maybe we'd even be able to catch some bigger fish to feed our bellies.

Around midday we went exploring again, this time to the south. We stumbled upon a large beehive inside an old dead tree. We'd seen our father do this a few times before. Smoke the bees out so we could steal their honey. We gathered as much dry wood as we could possibly find and placed it up against the tree where the bees had nested. We got stung a few times of course whenever we wandered too close to the hole where the hive was embedded, but we knew that it would all be worth it in the end.

Using a bunch of long dry grass as kindle, we lit it up with our newly acquired lighter. Within minutes, fire and smoke engulfed the entire bottom half of the tree. Some of the bees were already evacuating for their lives, but not enough for my sister's liking. So, she grabbed one of the burning logs and shoved it right into the hive's opening. That seemed to do the trick and very soon hundreds upon hundreds of confused wee bees were fleeing for their lives in every possible direction.

I just kept my distance and watched as my brave and unphased sister shoved her arm into the burning hole and yanked out the entire bees' nest. We took it away from the tree and smashed it to pieces. We then gathered up all the honey and wax inside and stashed them into one of our plastic carrier bags. It would serve us well as a tasty dinner desert treat for later that night.

We ended up back at the loch with a few hours to spare before sun down. We tried our best to catch some fish using our bottle traps and our make-shift hooks but didn't come close at all to catching anything. I think our coat hanger hooks were a wee bit too big for the fish in this particular loch. We left the bottle traps in place underneath the water though weighing them down with rocks. You just never knew what might lurk into them during the night and provide us with a nice, tasty breakfast snack.

That night we sat around the fire again and munched away on another two rabbits that my sister had caught in her snares. By the time we'd chewed up all the honey and beeswax our little bellies were full.

After our meal my sister lit up one of the cigarettes and smoked it. She did this without even coughing anymore. Yeah, she'd been smoking on and off for a while now. Since we were around eight years old, I think. She'd stolen her first packet of fags from the caretaker's office at school then pretty much forced our entire class to take a puff after she'd lit one during lunch break.

You'd have thought my father, who wasn't a smoker, would be furious. But as long as she didn't buy them with her own money or smoke them anywhere near the house, he seemed surprisingly fine with it. Like I said, it was amazing what my sister could get away with when it came to my father.

Back in the forest outside our shelter I declined to have anything to do with the smokes. I absolutely loathed the disgusting taste in my mouth and the foul, lingering smell on my clothes with a passion. I'd tried it once before, that time back at school when everyone else was forced to have a go, but once was enough for me.

My sister cracked open the vodka next and took a long, hard swig from the bottle. My father did like a drink or two every now and again, so it was no surprise that at least one of his little girls had taken up the habit. I didn't mind the alcohol though, especially when we were camping out on the cold dark nights. It always warmed me up while making me a wee bit more relaxed. It also gave me a cracking sleep, just so long as I didn't take too many sips or else it was a cracking headache too.

Again, my father didn't care what we did while out on our wild adventures. Whatever we found, gathered, or acquired out in the wilderness, we were free to do with and make use of, in any way we pleased or saw fit.

Chapter 4

The first thing we did when we awoke the next morning was run as fast as we could all the way back to the loch. To my sister's joy there were no new campers hanging around this time and, when we dived into the refreshing water to check our traps, we found that we'd caught a couple of little breakfast snacks, too, to our delighted surprise.

After we'd washed, swam, and dried ourselves down on the edge of the loch we made our way back to our hidden campsite again. Once there we speared our fish on little sticks and roasted them on the fire. After we'd eaten every single last piece of them we decided to go for another wee wander through the woods. This time to the east side.

On the verge of a small dipping valley, still within the perimeter of the forest, we came across another small tent, sitting way down in the belly of the valley. We crouched down low and kept a keen eye out for any movement. Nothing out of the ordinary happened or moved for a good twenty minutes, so we decided to sneak a little further down the valley and take a better look. Either the camper (or campers) were still asleep inside or, like us, they were out for a wander too in amongst the vast maze of trees and valleys. I hoped for the latter.

Again, we watched the tent for any sign of movement for at least another ten minutes. I started to get a nervous feeling in the pit of my tummy. I told my sister that we should just leave this place and go look somewhere else for our kicks and giggles, since this was to be our last full day out in the wild, fending for ourselves. But that curious magnetic force and pull from within my sister got the better of her once more and she refused to go anywhere until she, at the very least, knew what the hell was inside that damn tent.

Within moments of our argument, she'd moved closer towards another tree only a dozen yards away from the quiet campsite. She had a couple of small rocks in her hand and threw one, smack bang into the side of the tent. We both swiftly hid behind our trees. I waited for the sound of some enraged person to come howling out from within before bursting through the tent and out into the open, ready to throttle the culprits who'd damaged their property, but that sight nor sound never erupted.

My sister smiled and winked straight at me. Then she threw all of the small rocks and stones she was holding, all at once, bombarding the entire side of the tent in a shower of hard and violent attacks. No one yelled or came outside. Nothing moved from inside either. My sister took that as her queue to approach and investigate further. I duly followed but kept my distance of only a few trees behind her at all times.

She stood outside the zipped-up doorway. Fearlessly, she leaned in towards the zipper and gently slid it all the way down. The whole, entire time I kept imagining some crazy monster inside, perhaps even my father, who could suddenly yank my sister into the darkness to do unspeakable acts of bloody violence and terror to her body. My sister stuck her head further into the opened doorway. She hesitated for a moment before disappearing inside altogether.

I stood absolutely still, safe behind my tree yet frozen in a panic of fear of what she might find in there. When my sister failed to re-emerge after more than a minute, maybe two, even failing to make any damn sound or movement for that matter, I became very scared and anxious for her safety.

I swiftly swallowed my fear and called out her name. She never replied and the tent remained absolutely still. I took a deep breath and bit my lower lip. I'd have to go over there and investigate for myself. I inhaled deeply, then slowly but surely moved one foot in front of the other, my heart beating like a carnival drum.

I approached the tent, peeled back the flap of the door and peered inside.

To my blatant surprise I couldn't see anyone in there at all. Nothing and no one. *What the hell?* I couldn't believe it. Just some big old dark green rucksack along with some scattered camping materials, tins of food, bottles of water, and a big cosy old sleeping bag.

I called my sister's name again. *Where the hell could she be? Where the bloody hell could she have gone now?*

I stepped all the way inside with my heart now firmly planted at the roof of my mouth.

Suddenly, my sister pounced up at me from underneath the bulky old sleeping bag. She roared like a bear, almost frightening the morning breakfast out of me. I screamed in shock and fell off balance. I tried to stop myself from toppling over but couldn't prevent myself from falling hard, right onto the side of the tent, piercing myself all the way through the material and ripping right through it all together.

My sister fell back onto the comfy sleeping bag and rolled around from side to side, belly-laughing hysterically as I landed on the ground of the soft forest dirt outside. I cursed her name over and over, then called her a few other nasty things too that I wasn't particularly proud of in the moment, but that just made her erupt with laughter even more.

Then another sound bellowed out from the other side of the clearing, just beyond the thick row of trees there. A new foreign sound made by neither me or my sister.

"What the fuck are you doing to my tent?"

It was that distant but angry voice that finally made my sister shut the hell up then sit up more alert than I'd ever seen her.

I quickly glanced over to my left and in the direction where I'd heard the strong, angry male voice coming from. Through the trees I could just about see a tall, well-built man, much larger than my father and wearing jeans, a thick jacket, and a woolly hat. He started running towards me.

"HEY. What the fuck are you doing to my tent? That's my fucking tent, you little fucking shit!"

I glanced at my sister through the huge ripped hole. She glanced back at me and yelled run, or at least that's what I think she did – Perhaps she just mouthed it. Everything happened so fast. So that's exactly what I did. I clambered onto my feet and ran back up the steep forest hill, fast as I could, back the way I'd came.

When I'd made it at least half way up, I took a quick peek back just to check where my sister was at more than anything and how far she might be behind. My heart skipped two beats though when she wasn't anywhere to be seen. The man was though. And he was climbing up the steep slope like a raging monster bat out of hell right after me. Either my sister was still hiding in the tent and the man hadn't seen or heard her, or, she'd ran in the opposite direction, making the crazed man choose. Me or her. One or the other. Either way, the enraged man was chasing after me.

I ran as fast as my wee legs could carry me. I'd almost made it to the very top of the wooded valley too when the crazy, angry man, scrambling ever closer towards me, took a wild dive and grabbed a firm hold of my left ankle. I fell to the ground with an unhealthy thud, face first and smacking my forehead hard against the bottom of a tree trunk directly in front of me.

The angry man didn't care too much about my wellbeing though. He climbed furiously right on top of my tiny body and turned me harshly onto my back so that we were eye to eye, his snarling face inches from mine.

"Where the hell do you think you're going, huh? You little shit." the man spat. I felt too dazed, sore, and confused to answer him back or even look him in the eye for that matter. So, I did what I always did in stressful situations like these: I began to cry.

"You destroyed my tent, you little vandal. Where the hell are your parents, huh? They around here too? They know that you go around causing criminal damage to people's bloody properties, huh?" continued the angry man, still snarling and spitting and drooling all over me.

Finally, he climbed back up onto his feet before dragging me up onto mine. I tried to cover my face with my hands as the tears and sobs poured out of me, but he kept pulling and slapping them away.

"Shut the hell up. You're not hurt, you little brat."

I kept crying which seemed to make the man even angrier. He put his hands on my shoulders and shook me hard.

"Stop your bloody whining, you little shit. Now where the hell are you staying around here, huh? Who's responsible for you out here, huh? Take me to them."

Suddenly the man howled out to the high heavens with such agonizing pain that I ceased crying immediately. It was such an unexpected reaction on his part that it left me utterly lost for words. When he yowled out again with even greater agony, I finally opened my eyes just in time to see him collapse onto the floor in a crumpled heap.

Standing right beside him was my sister. In her hands was a long, sturdy and powerful log. She'd cracked the thing with all her strength right into the side of the man's knee cap and, while he'd held his leg in excruciating pain, still howling to the unseen moon and heavens, she'd smashed him again. This time on his other knee. He'd fallen to the ground like a huge sack of sweet potatoes as his legs folded and buckled with the weight of his upper body on their newly broken frame.

The angry, howling man rolled around on the dirt and mud, clutching at both of his knees. My sister didn't stop there though. Not by a long shot. She cracked him again and again with another hard-swinging blow, this time against his elbow and then the side of his arm. The man cried in agony. She swung again, now against his other arm. He tried to raise his hand to protect himself and dull the blow but she smashed him so hard on the outer forearm that the snap echoed throughout the surrounding trees. She'd completely shattered his forearm. Bloodied white bone poked out from within his flesh.

I was about to yell at her to stop, when she hit him one more time. Right on top of his skull. There was a healthy crack and the man seemed to calm down quite suddenly. His painful cries for help and for my sister to stop, swiftly subsided. He didn't fall unconscious by any means, but more into a groggy, retarded daze.

My sister went to strike him again, clearly enjoying herself, caught up in the exhilarating and maddening violence of the moment.

This time I shouted "Enough!"

She looked at me with a coy expression before smiling warmly and lowering her arms to finally relax.

***

I helped my sister drag the groggy man over towards the nearest tree. She then ordered me back down to his tent and told me to try and find some rope to tie him up with. If I couldn't find any rope then I was to tie all of the man's clothes together and use that for a rope instead.

I found some rope though. Lots of it. Like a climber's rope, thin but sturdy, in one of his rucksacks. When I made my way back up the hill I saw my sister strike the man across the face with her log again. I didn't like it, but if I wasn't there to stop her then what the hell could I do? When she saw me coming back up the hill she threw the log down onto the ground and told me to hurry the hell up.

We tied the full length of rope around both the tree and the groggy man's body. His face and head were much more bloodied, bruised, and swollen than I remembered but, again, I didn't say anything to my sister about these new wounds.

For our final night of camping out in the forest, we decided to leave our secluded shelter and move into the man's tent down at the bottom of the forest valley. It was a nice-sized tent with a good, cosy sleeping bag that could easily fit both me and my sister inside, no problem. Plus, we could be closer to the man and keep a better eye on him from this new base.

I wasn't sure what we we're gonna do with him, to be honest, when we finally came to leave this place, but my sister seemed to think that it would be a good idea to keep him tied up like that until my father came for us the next day. Perhaps he could somehow iron the misunderstanding out and everything would be right as rain again.

We started a new fire outside the man's tent, then proceeded to eat the majority of his food. He was still very much unconscious up there on the top of the valley. And after a few hours of not hearing him utter a single groan or even shout out for any more help, I began to fear the worst. I was about to go up and see him, perhaps even throw some water in his face or shake him awake, when just as we were finishing off a second can of rice pudding from his dwindling stash, the man began groaning and moaning out for help just like he'd done a few hours earlier.

My sister instantly grabbed her log. However, I swiftly placed my hand upon hers and motioned for her to leave it be. The sun was still up, perhaps only an hour or so away from setting for another day, so I didn't need any extra light in order to make my way back up the valley.

I took an opened tin of baked beans along with a spoon. I thought he might be quite hungry by now and that the food could also act as some kind of a peace offering between us. I cautiously approached the man as my sister kept a muted distance a few yards behind. He still had both his eyes fully closed yet he was groaning for help, almost delirious but not too loud. The left side of his face, especially his left eye, was swollen to almost three times its normal size. It looked utterly hideous and ridiculous at the same time, like it somehow wasn't real and someone had snuck into the woods just before my arrival to cake this gruesome, horror-film, makeup effect upon him. Had my sister really done that to his face? She had well and truly done him over a cracker that's for sure. God only knew what state his legs were in.

The man must have heard us coming. He stopped his groans and turned his attention towards me. His right eye opened, but his left did not. I was slightly taken aback by how freakishly unhuman he appeared. He seemed more like some Frankenstein monster than any average human being.

"Please... Please untie me, little girl." The man croaked through his broken mouth and jaw. I didn't reply. I just gently shook my head as I stood in front of him.

"I need an ambulance. I need to get to a hospital," he said, struggling to speak and dribbling every time he opened his mouth. I thought his jaw must have been broken. I glanced at my sister who stood half hidden and half revealing herself beside another tree. I focused my attention back to the mumbling man.

"I think… at least one of my knees… or legs… are broken. My arm too. I'm scared that it might get infected if I stay out here like this any longer."

I watched him carefully and listened to his pleas but I said absolutely nothing.

"Please. Just untie me and help me get out of this forest. I won't get you, or your sister, is it? I won't get either of you into any trouble. Please, just help me… Or at least go and get me some help. Please. I beg you. It hurts so much."

I raised the opened can of beans and swirled the spoon around inside the thick, lumpy orange contents a few times. I then scooped out a spoonful of raw, sloppy beans and moved it towards the man's face. I told him to eat, but he just sighed and looked at me like I was some kind of idiot.

"I'm not hungry. I just need some help. A doctor or an ambulance…before it gets too dark… Please."

I told him there was nothing I could do for him until my father came for us the following day. He'd have to wait until then and see what my father decided was best for everyone. The man didn't seem to like that answer. But instead of getting angry though he just closed his eyes, lowered his head, and started to sob again.

"Please..." he begged. "Please. I have a wife… and a little girl. She's just a bit younger than you are now. Please. I really want to get back home to see them."

Ignoring his pleas once more I crouched down to his eye level and moved the spoonful of beans closer to his mouth. An inch or so away from his lips. With a sturdier tone and sounding more like my sister, I told him to eat the beans; this made him finally erupt in a bout of anger. He butted, spat, and hissed the spoonful of beans away, knocking it out of my hands and onto the dark ground.

"I don't want any food you stupid little bitch. I want a fucking ambulance. Do you hear me? I want some fucking medical attention!" the man screamed in frustration.

I stumbled and fell back onto my bum with the fright of his sudden outburst and change in tone from grovelling and pleading to complete and utter rage. That rage reminded me of my father for a beat, but not the grovelling though.

Suddenly my sister leapt out from her hiding place behind a nearby tree. Before I could even protest she had taken the can of beans from my grasp and poured the contents all over the man's head. Then she began smothering the beans all over his face, too, with the palm of her hand, rather too violently for my liking.

The man roared in pain as my sister palmed, patted, and slapped the cold beans all over his swollen jaw and face. When she was done she kicked his broken arm hard before laughing at how ridiculous he now looked.

Silent and ashamed, I gazed on as the man began sobbing once again. My sister cursed more obscenities right into his face before kicking his broken knee this time. That was the final straw. I couldn't take the torturing and suffering any longer. I stood up and told my sister to cease her abuse immediately. I had to put my arm right across her chest just to stop her from stomping all over the man's leg for a second time. My sister just glared at me like I'd deeply insulted her intelligence, but after a slight hesitation, she gradually backed away.

I apologized to the man for my sister's behaviour. I tried to explain to him that my sister was just very protective of me and that she didn't like it when people tried to hurt or scare me. Well, everyone except my father that is—which I didn't say out loud, of course.

I told the man that there was nothing more I could do for him until my father arrived. I said I would bring him another can of food later that night and when I did, he should just be grateful and eat whatever I gave him and not try anything like that again.

Chapter 5

I really didn't think that the man would make it through the night. He refused, quietly and submissively the next time, to eat or drink anything else that I offered him, until eventually, we just decided to leave him in peace for the rest of the night.

We sat around our fire, cooked, and ate the rest of his food, and drank a few mouthfuls of the vodka we'd taken from the women's tent before passing out, snuggled up together inside the man's sleeping bag.

In the morning we climbed up the hill to see him again. He didn't seem to be moving too much and I really feared the worst. It was hard to say if he was even breathing anymore. But when my sister kicked his broken arm, he immediately jolted awake. He glanced up at us with a look of downright defeat and despair. I'd never seen such an expression like that from anyone before in my life.

He didn't utter a single word either, even when I asked him how he was feeling and if he was hungry yet. He just gently shook his head before turning his swollen eyes away to look anywhere else but in our direction. In a way, I actually felt glad that he didn't want any food because my sister and I had eaten the lot of his and we'd have to go hunting again, or swimming into the loch to see if our fish traps were still working and had caught some more fish.

I'd brought a half bottle of water with us and forced it up against his lips. Thankfully, he drank a few gulps without any protest, which I took as a good sign. I told him that we'd be back soon. That we were only going for a morning swim in the nearby loch and then to the outskirts of the forest to see if our father was waiting for us at the meeting point he'd told us to be at.

My sister and I were just about to head off through the trees when the man raised his head all of a sudden. His eyes widened and his eyebrows rose. I swear, for one fracture of a second, a smile threatened to broaden across his hideously swollen and bloodied face too. I wasn't sure what the hell was wrong with him at first, but when I heard some branches moving, then the sound of leaves and twigs crunching and cracking behind us, my heart stopped again. We had more company in the woods. Before either my sister or myself could turn around to see just who the hell might be sneaking up on us, the man was already crying out for their aid and assistance.

"Police. POLICE! Oh, thank Christ, it's the police. Jesus Christ. Help me God. Please, please help me. Dear God, am I so happy to see you Officer. Thank the Lord. Thank the bloody Lord."

The man gave out a shuddering sigh of relief. My sister was the first of us to turn swiftly around and glance at the uniformed police officer edging slowly towards us. Instantly, she smiled and gave him a warm friendly wave of recognition to the police man.

It was our father, of all people, and he was wearing his full police chief uniform, which wasn't like him at all when he was out and about in the wilderness. I neither smiled nor waved. The man though—wow—he looked absolutely broken and distraught when he realized that we knew the approaching police man. He almost gagged too when he saw my sister waving and smiling at him, showing him so much love. He looked like he was about to have a stroke, just to add to his growing list of grievances.

"No, please... Mr. police man, please... Please, help me," the man continued half-heartedly. But his hope of a simple and uncomplicated rescue was draining thick and fast from his defeated body language.

Our father emerged from the trees and into the small clearing where my sister and I still stood, rooted to the dirt, and where the tied and beaten man, sat, still bound against the tree.

"Awright ma girls. Still alive ah sees. Very good. No bad for yer first time oot in the big bad wilderness aw by yersels, eh?"

Our unusually cheery father then turned his attention towards the tied and beaten man.

"What's aw this then?" my father asked like he'd caught us red handed eating cookies right before dinner. I tried to explain what had happened to the best of my ability. Not leaving anything out, except for the drinking of vodka and the burning down of the two seemingly-nice women's tent over by the loch. Although, it was fair to assume that if he knew about this scenario, then he also knew about the two women too.

My sister remained absolutely silent, like she usually did in these situations. She always let me do the talking, even though we were in this situation because of her actions, not mine. When I'd finally finished filling Dad in on everything that had happened, he gently stepped towards me. I tried not to flinch and firmly held my ground. I couldn't actually tell if he was going to strike me across the jaw with the back of his hand like he sometimes did or softly stroke the back of my head, like he sometimes did too. His mood could change that fast.

To my relief he took the latter action. He stroked his hand over the back of my head and through my long, jet-black hair. It was a good feeling. It meant that everything was going to be okay.

"It's awright, ma wee dolls. Ah saw the whole thing yesterday fae behind they trees over there. Ye dinnae have tae explain yourselves tae me, ma wee darlings. Ah saw this paedo fuckwit chasing ye's. Trying tae grab ye, then pinning ye doon tae dae god knows whit. Assaulting a poor wee, innocent girl oot in the middle of naywhere like some cowardly fuckin sex offender."

My dad shook his head for effect before spitting at the man.

"No. No," the man protested, coughing and spluttering out. "That's not what happened here. And if you were really watching, then you'd know the truth. You'd know the truth, officer," He cried, raising his voice.

My dad suddenly tensed up. He ceased the soothing, stroking motion of my hair.

"Shut it you, ye cunt," he snarled.

He took his hand away from me and stepped slowly—intimidatingly slowly—right up to the man, so that he stood directly over him, his groin almost touching the man's face.

"Are ye calling ma daughter a fuckin liar likes?"

The man almost choked with fear. He shook his head. He tried to clear his throat.

"No. I'm not saying that, sir. I'm not calling anyone a liar here. Not at all."

"Fuckin sir, is it noo? Ye fucking shitebag paedo prick."

"I'm just saying that..." the man mumbled on, clearly in pain the more he worked his jaw. "...this has all been one, big, huge, misunderstanding. And if you could just kindly take me to a hospital...."

Dad feigned a kick to the man's broken leg. The man yelped and flinched at the fake attack while Dad just smiled sadistically and chuckled.

"...or, or ta a police station. Then I'm sure this can all be resolved quickly. I promise. Then I'll just go my separate way...I won't say a single word, not one bloody word, about anything that's happened here..."

Dad crouched down in front of the man, painfully slow. He made himself eye level with the man and his one good eye who was shaking uncontrollably.

"You wullnae say anything aboot what happened here?" Dad said coldly and softly, almost in a whisper. "What fuckin happened here likes? Al tell ye whit fuckin happened here, ye paedo fuckin baw-jawed bastard. If it wusnae for ma wee, brave, quick-thinking, other daughter, knocking you auf yur fucking perch, ya silly fucktard, then baeth of them would nay doot be lying raped, deed, and buried in the ground right about noo, is that no the truth of it pal, aye?"

"No, no, no, no, no," sobbed the man. "That's not what was going to happen here," he said, weeping wildly. "They destroyed my tent. They stole my food. I only wanted to..."

"Ye only wanted tae what ye cunt, huh? Ye only wanted tae what?"

"To scare her. To teach her a lesson. To take her back to her parents and tell them what she'd done to my possessions."

"Tae scare her, aye. Tae teach her a lesson. Yur four times her size ye fucking prick."

The man continued to sob hard.

"Bet ye wished yid just left them be and let them run back off intae the woods noo, aeh?" Dad said with another callous chuckle. He took a deep breath. He stood back up and turned to me and my sister.

"Go oan then, girls. Auf ye's get noo. Ye ken the way hame. Av left two fresh rabbits oot on the kitchen worktop. Pick some veggies fae the garden and start making a soup for dinner the night, awright."

I didn't look at Dad. I just stared at the scared, sobbing man, sitting down in front of him, looking like a frightened animal caught up in the biggest trap of his life. Somewhere deep inside I knew dad was going to kill this man, then bury his body out here in the woods somewhere where he'd never, ever be found again, before getting rid of all evidence and traces that he was ever there in the first place. I wanted to tell dad to leave the man alone. To just let him go or get him to a hospital like he so desperately wanted. He was harmless. And I was pretty convinced that he'd never say a single word about anything that happened here to anyone, even to the authorities. I mean, it was his word against two, innocent, wee teenage girls and a policeman after all.

But that cold hard stare from my father. I'd seen it before and it always chilled me to the bone. He wasn't someone you could just question for the hell of without there being some kind of consequences and repercussions. And then there's the fact that he'd been so nice to us—so proud of us both for surviving out here in the wild for three nights on the trot. Pride was a feeling that was usually alien from my father, but when you did receive even just a kindle of it, and he praised you and he made you feel so good about yourself in just a few short moments, I always felt ten feet taller afterwards. So, you could imagine how my sister must've been feeling.

"Oan ye's go then. Chop, chop," said dad, ushering us away. "Al deal wi this mess."

I finally met my father's stare but his steely gaze was almost impossible to hold. So, I quickly nodded and turned away. I glanced at my sister and motioned her with a swift nod in the direction that we should be moving in. Before she even took one step, she asked my father outright if she could stay behind and help him out or at least watch and learn something from what he was about to do. I could almost hear my dad's heart swelling with more pride than it could surely hold in that moment. He'd almost, but not quite, let out the faintest of smiles. Almost.

"Nay chance, ya wee bampot. Noo get a fuckin move oan and get that bludy pot of soup ready for me coming hame. Comprende."

My sister nodded and let out a disappointed sigh like she'd been denied to stay out a wee bit longer after dark. She took a hold of my hand and we both started walking off through the trees, towards the south side of the forest. Neither of us looked back and neither of us talked about what happened there that day again. Well, not openly and out loud that was for sure.

Chapter 6

We didn't go to school anymore. Dad just kept us both holed up at the farmhouse all day and night, while making us read all kinds of books, fiction and nonfiction, either from his own collection or stuff that he'd pick up for us at the nearest library. Every time he gave us a book he told us to read it by the end of the week and then write him an essay in our own words regarding what the book was about, what we'd learned from reading it, and how we could implement what we'd learned into our own lives. On some occasions he'd also ask us how we could make the book better, like if we'd wrote it ourselves. What would we change? How would we tell that story?

What were the books you might ask? Nothing I ever wanted to read for my own pleasure, that was for damn sure. It was usually just whatever nonsense he happened to be in the mood for himself. Like books about poisonous and edible plants. Survival books. Mountain Climbing and survivalist biographies. Or fiction books that he'd enjoyed reading himself while growing up. Last week it was Cormac McCarthy's Child of God. The week before it was Crime and Punishment. This week it was Pan by Knut Hamsun. Surprise, surprise, there was usually some kind of survival theme in the subtext and a man was always the main protagonist and author.

I remembered a rare friend of mine from school loaned me a copy of his old, fantasy adventure book. It was called *The Princess of Mars* and I absolutely adored it. This was the kind of book children my age should be reading. Apparently, there were another seven or eight follow up books in the series but I never got around to reading any of them. Here's why: a few months back, dad had both me and my sister yanked out of school. A school that was based in the town closest to us, fifteen miles away.

It was when one of our teachers, Mr. Morris, had become suspicious of our after-school lives and activities. He'd began noticing more and more marks and bruises regularly appearing on exposed parts of our bodies over the ongoing weeks and months. I think he believed that our seemingly good and decent Chief of police, Christian father, was up to no good and beating us most nights, black and blue, back at our farmhouse.

Pretty big and wild accusations to be swinging around such a small, quiet town and against such a highly respected town official. To tell you the truth, yes, our father did strike us from time to time, perhaps a couple of times a year, but he always did it in such a clever way as to never leave a mark, especially on any part of our bodies that might be exposed to the public. (Our school had a swimming pool.) But the marks our teacher saw were always, hand on heart, from our survival adventures and extreme camping expeditions at the weekends, out in the wild with him or by ourselves.

When my dad finally met with the teachers to discuss the complaint, he proved his case undoubtedly by having them witness my sister and I building a shelter from scratch out in the school playing fields, while also digging for water, showing how to plant seeds and grow vegetables, and searching for edible plants to eat around the school grounds.

When the teachers started enthusiastically applauding after we'd made a fire practically out of nothing but a couple of old dry sticks, the complaint against him was firmly dropped. The other teachers all then congratulated him on how proud he must be at bringing up two brilliant and abled daughters all on his own, and how they wished the other parents and children at the school adopted just a few of his philosophies and teachings instead of just plumping their kids in front of iPads, iPhones and smart TVs after school hours.

Of course, he never mentioned a jot about his philosophies and musings regarding the imminent and looming end of the world and apocalypse that he believed, without a shadow of a doubt, was fast approaching and was about to wipe out every single one of these unprepared, gullible and idiotic people. Or why there happened to be a slightly higher case of unexplained and unsolved deaths, animal and human, in this particular region of the beautiful Scottish Highlands.

Unsatisfied though by his colleague's swift dismissal of his concerns and light allegations, Mr. Morris also started subtly questioning us about the whereabouts of our mother too and why she wasn't around anymore? When was the last time we'd seen her? And where she might be now? Which of course was another big no-no, once my sister had reported his enquiries back to my father.

A few weeks later, dad told the school that he was sending us away to live with our mother down in Glasgow as he didn't have the time or the resources to look after us anymore. And from that day on he began to home school us at the farmhouse, away from the prying eyes of any interfering outsiders.

Two months later, we conveniently heard that some rather indecent images of children were found on our dear old teacher, Mr. Morris's home computer. My dad of course took great pleasure in arresting him shortly after, right in front of the entire school assembly, before dragging him off to jail. Never to be seen nor heard from again.

Since then and on some very rare occasions, if someone who we happened to know from our school days randomly bumped into us out in the country, child or adult, or up at the farmhouse, we were always told to say that we were just up visiting our father for a few days and going back to Glasgow soon to be with our mother again.

But that only happened one time when my sister and I were out trekking down the coast that stretches north and south for miles and miles in either direction at the back of our house. We were looking for crabs, mussels, and oysters for dinner and bumped into another of our old teachers from school, who just happened to be out and about for a casual hike with her own family. We'd forgotten that it was a school holiday that week, so lucky for us our story made out.

Which brings me back to *The Princess of Mars*.

Back when we were attending school on a regular basis and we had to socialize with the other kids, there was one particular boy I was very fond of: Jamie Brewster. He had the most beautiful blue eyes and mop-like blonde hair that fell down to just below his cheekbones.

Jamie was the one who'd loaned me the book. A book I also had to keep well hidden from both my father and sister. I remembered fondly too that Jamie used to call me 'his Princess of Mars' which made my sister want to vomit and gag every time she heard it in the playground. But me, I adored him for it. And at the end of the day I think she was just jealous that someone had taken a shine to me instead of her.

Jamie and I used to hang around a lot at break time, playing snap cards, skipping around the school grounds, playing hopscotch, and running around pretending we were characters from the book. We did everything together during school breaks until, one day, my sister decided it would be most fun to set his beautiful blonde hair on fire.

Thankfully, she only managed to singe a fistful size clump of his beautiful blonde locks as she held him down by the throat with one hand behind the PE changing rooms one rainy afternoon before setting his hair on fire with the lighter in her other hand.

Running to Jamie's aid I was quick enough to wrestle the lighter from my sister's hands, before pouring the contents of my lunchtime orange juice all over his burning head of hair to put out the flames before she had time to do any permanent damage. I made him promise not to tell on my sister though. And to explain to the teachers, along with his parents, that he had found the lighter in the changing rooms and accidentally set fire to his own hair. Reluctantly, he agreed. More due to the fear of what my sister might do to him while he slept at night more than anything else, should he ever confess what really happened that day. He also swore never to speak to me again. And so, I never got to read any more in the *Princess of Mars* book series

A few months later, my sister and I were both pulled out of the school, which by that point Jamie's new skinhead haircut was beginning to grow back once more, which I was extremely grateful for. But he never did call me his Princess of Mars again.

Chapter 7

I only brought up once the topic of whatever happened to our mother and why she'd left our family home. I think I must have been around nine or ten years old at the time. No sooner than I had asked that burning question when my father then proceeded to lift me by the roots of my hair, dangle me in front of his face, and shout all kinds of obscenities and foul abuse in my direction, mainly about how I should mind my own business and stop asking such stupid questions. Although, his words weren't quite as politely put as that.

From that day onwards, I learned my lesson to never ever bring up the subject of my mother again, unless my father mentioned it first. Which of course he never did. Then one day, while my sister and I were at home alone and my father was out at work, we discovered a secret basement chamber underneath the house. A series of secret, cellar-like rooms that we had no idea actually existed.

I was lying on the couch, trying to catch up on my weekly reading assignment, and my sister was meant to be outside hanging out the days washing and feeding the chickens in the back garden when, out of nowhere, a bloodied head of one of the chickens landed right on my lap, smearing plenty of blood and entrails all over my white t-shirt and book—dad's book.

I'd never felt more furious before in my life. I knew exactly who was going to get the blame for this, too, once dad discovered the state of one of his books. My sister was clearly his favourite, so already she would be in the clear from all wrong-doing.

I stood up. A rush of blood went straight to my head. My sister remained standing where she was, smirking and grinning as if to say *what the hell are you gonna do about it*? Which infuriated me even more. I hated it when she entered one of these mischievous and playful moods.

It wasn't my finest moment, but I went for her nonetheless. Even though I knew she was stronger than me. I knew she was a better fighter than me, but I didn't care. I grabbed her by the roots of her hair and shoulders and began wrestling her, every which way I could. All over the living room. On top of tables. Onto the couch. Over chairs. One chair even collapsed in pieces when I threw her onto it.

I don't know how, but we ended up fighting and brawling out in the hallway. My energy and strength were dwindling to almost zero. Scratch marks, blood, and bruises covered most of our bodies and faces. I'd definitely given as good as I'd gotten on that occasion. Even my sister was impressed by my efforts, she later admitted.

Still, we wrestled against the hallway wall, pushing and pulling the other up towards the kitchen on the opposite side. On the other wall, right beside the staircase, stood one of dad's beautiful, old oak book cases, filled with all his favourite books and the ones that he'd make us read over and over again until our eyes cried blood. My sister threw me head-first into that bookcase, sending most of those books flying this way and that.

My head throbbed hard as I fell back onto the floor, almost unconscious. My sister wasn't done yet though, not by a long shot, and went to wrap her arms around my neck, putting me into some kind of sleeper hold.

That's when it happened: the huge, heavy, old oak bookcase, along with the entire contents of its hundred or so books, came crashing down upon us. When we finally wriggled free from underneath the chaotic mess, we both just sat there, stunned to silence at what we'd found.

Lying behind the book case was a small, hidden doorway. It fell absolutely flush with the wall. So, with the old bookcase propped securely up against it, nobody else was to be any the wiser that a secret door was actually there.

We both looked at each other and nodded, silently agreeing that we should go inside to further investigate. The slim door had no handle but it was unlocked, and with a slight push it led us into a tiny wee room tucked nicely beneath the main staircase of the house.

The room was so dark inside but my sister soon found a light switch by fondling the walls. She turned it on to reveal a steep, narrow staircase leading all the way down to a huge iron door at the very bottom foundation of the house. On the wall beside the first step down, a long and thick rusted key hung from a single hook.

My sister nudged me to grab the key. I took it and cautiously moved down the stairs with my sister behind. Neither one of us uttered a single word; our previous fight and feud scattered to the wind like dust. We moved ever closer towards the iron door. Apart from the main lock, there were three huge, thick bolts sitting upon the door. One at the top. One in the middle and one at the very bottom.

I couldn't help but wonder if this was to keep someone from getting in or to stop someone from getting out. I placed the key inside the lock. I had to push it hard and wriggle it about half a dozen times before it slotted in. We then pushed open the door together. It made the loudest and most unnatural groan I'd ever heard, sending a shiver right through my spine, from top to bottom.

Inside, I'd never witnessed an eerie darkness like it. Feeling our way around the cold, hard edges of the cellar walls for any light switches just inside the doorway, we weren't able find any. Before we stepped fully inside this new dark place, I told my sister to wait for me at the iron door for just one minute while I ran back up the stairs and fetched a torch or some kind of light source for us.

I knew she wouldn't wait. Unlike me, she was absolutely fearless in these situations. Forever the avid adventurer. She didn't need light to stop her from having a good explore of a pitch-black place.

From the living room cupboard, I grabbed one of the long, thick candles and a lighter that my dad stored there in case of a power cut. I hurried back down to the old iron door at the bottom of the steep, narrow staircase. As I expected, my sister wasn't anywhere to be seen.

As I lit the candle inside the doorway I called her name. She didn't reply. The candle light lit up a small portion of a long, winding, square corridor, which branched away to the right of the iron door. Here, there were various pitch-black doorways leading into other rooms scattered along the corridor's length before it took another sharp turn to the right, way up ahead.

I called out for my sister again. This time she answered from the darkness. She emerged at the far end of the shadowy corridor. She told me to come to her quickly. She'd found something in one of the gloomy, empty rooms but she needed a light now to see it properly.

I hurried towards her, but careful enough to shield the flickering candle flame with the palm of my hand from the passing stale air. I found my sister standing outside one of the rooms. She took the lighted candle from me as I approached and stepped a little further inside.

The weak flame gradually lit up the room. We could make out an old toilet and sink first on the right. There was an old fireplace, too, but it looked like it had not been used in many years.

In the far corner of the room lay a shabby, old single mattress. It still had some aged covers lying upon it and a strange, shallow bulge in its middle. My first thought was that someone—possibly a small child—might be sleeping underneath. But I quickly shook those thoughts from my mind. The bulge must be from some old pillows or hidden objects under the covers. What else could it be?

In the other far corner of the dark room, opposite from where we were standing, was a large, solid white freezer. As my eyes and ears adjusted, I heard the faint hum coming from its motor. I made a quick glance at my sister. No further words were spoken between us. My sister then made her way towards the old mattress and the covers, and I towards the freezer.

I stopped by the ancient sink and turned on the single tap there. No water came out. I checked the toilet too. It was also bone dry and when I flushed it, no water came out from the cistern. I then heard my sister make a little gasp.

When I turned around, she was already beside the mattress. She'd pulled all the covers away to reveal something crumpled and dirty underneath. Something I didn't entirely recognize at first in the dim shadows of light. But something that looked very unnatural.

I moved towards the mattress with my sister standing over it. On closer inspection it looked like an animal carcass. It didn't feel right though. Why wasn't I satisfied with the idea that it might be that? Why was I then thinking that it might be something much more tragic than a dead, meaningless animal—something more sinister, more shocking?

I finally reached the mattress and stood beside my sister. I took a deep breath. My sister remained cool, calm, emotionless, unphased. She just continued to stare down at the *thing*.

Finally, I could see what it was in the dull light. It was an old, rotten, human Skeleton. From what I could tell, remembering the biology books I'd read in the past, both at home and at school, it was that of a female. It was a rough guess, but the sciatic notch in the female pelvis is usually wider than that of a male one. Also, the pelvic inlet of a female is usually oval in shape, just like this skeleton, while a man's can be kind of heart-shaped. That's what I remembered from the books anyhow.

My sister was even less sure than me, but she seemed to agree with my conclusion. I wondered out loud who she might have been. *How long had her remains been down here? When had she died? Could this even be our own mother?*

My sister just gave me a look of utter daggers and disgust and told me not to say anything so stupid like that again. She must have been a bad person, my sister finally stated, or had annoyed dad in some way. Enough to deserve such a dark, miserable life down in this cellar. Why else would she be here?

We turned our attention to the freezer. We looked at each other again. With the power still running from a cable that ran all the way up the wall and through the ceiling to the house above, whatever lay inside it couldn't be good.

We approached the freezer together. I didn't want to, but my sister insisted and led the way. I just wanted to get the hell out of this place. Lock the door, throw away the key, and never ever think about this cellar and its horror show of contents ever again.

My sister reached the freezer. She waited until I'd stood beside her before attempting to slide her fingers into the cracks of the lid to lift it open. It opened with ease. A waft of freezing cold air seeped out all around us. We peered inside at the exact same time. My sister didn't flinch. I jolted back and covered my mouth with both hands just to stop myself from crying out.

Inside, the freezer was full of dozens upon dozens of dead, frozen, little, new-born babies. God only knew how long they'd been left in there for. Probably for as long as the skeleton had laid dead, was my first thought. But I was at a loss for words. I'd never seen anything more terrifying or more horrific before in my entire life. Until my dying day I doubt that I'd ever see a site quite like that again.

My sister closed the lid. She told me that we had to get the hell out of there. Lock the iron door. Put back the key. Tidy up the bookshelf, the books, the hallway, and the living room, too—put it all back together like nothing had ever happened. Dad could never find out what we'd discovered down in that cellar. He could never know that we'd been in there full stop.

Chapter 8

One weekend, I truly did get to see my father's monstrous and psychotic tendencies in the cold, hard flesh. I knew that he'd killed at least three times before in his life. The woman in the cellar, who my sister and I never ever mentioned or spoke about again. The road rage incident a few years back with the driver he'd beaten to death right in front of our very eyes, whilst my sister and I watched with wildly different emotions. Then the camper/hiker in the forest from the other week—although I could never be one hundred percent certain of his fate, I just went with my general gut feeling which told me that he was now food for the plants, trees, and insects in some dark and remote region of the forest a few miles along the coast from our home.

Of course, these were the only deaths that I knew about thus far. I had no idea about my father's actions before I was born or even before I started forming any kind of memories, and anything he did out of my line of sight and sound was another black void of mystery to me. So, to say that there had only been two killings on his part since the beginning of his existence on the planet was a great misconception and a wide berth of naivety on my part.

I remembered I was outside feeding our small army of chickens in the back garden on a sunny Saturday, mid-June afternoon. In fact, it could have been the weekend of the longest day of the year or, perhaps, the weekend before. It's hard to think about the details now.

My father suddenly stepped out from the shadows of the back-kitchen doorway and told me that we were driving down to Glasgow in exactly twenty minutes time to partake in a new survival exercise, and to get a general taste of how the plague of humanity lived.

He told me to go and fetch my sister who had been out fishing down at one of the rocky beaches nearby for most of the afternoon, and that we were both to bring our hunting knives with us for the drive down along with our wits. We were also to leave any 'silly fucking questions' that we may have regarding what might happen down in Glasgow, back in the house.

Down on the beach, my sister looked most excited when I told her the news. Her eyes even glistened as she sliced and gutted another fish she'd recently caught from the cold, calm sea, casually adding it to the basket of dozens of other dead fish she'd caught and gutted that day.

As we drove through the late evening sunshine, first driving down miles upon miles of B roads through the secluded mountains, lochs, and glens before emerging onto the bigger and better laid out A roads, dad told us some stories about Glasgow and the upcoming apocalypse that would one day hit the city harder than any other place on God's green Earth.

"When the end comes, Glasgae will be the first fuckin place tae turn oan itsel. No doot aboot that. It's the biggest cesspit of human filth, decay and misery, by far on this shitehole of an Island. All the scum of Scotland seems tae wash up on its dirty, rancid streets at some point. When the end does come, it certainly wullnae be a place that'll be fuckin missed, that's for sure. No like Edinbara. Nay fuckin chance. Noo there's a city that will last the test of time. Solid as a fuckin rock that city wi its magnificent castle and aw its auld toon streets—solid as the fuckin rock it was built upon. When the shit truly does hit the fan, if you're no up in the Highlands like us smart cunts, learning tae live off the land and survive wi nothing in your pocket but your savy and wits, then your next fuckin option is tae locate the biggest, baddest, fuck off castle you can find and hoard yourself up in there for as long as ye can. And that's whit half the fuckin city will be tryin tae dae when the time comes. Every cunt in the city fightin over that fuckin castle. It'll be a bloodbath."

I wanted to ask more about this Edinburgh place. Of course, I'd seen pictures of it, just like I'd seen the pictures of Glasgow at school. And it did look mightily spectacular. Especially with its roaming populated hills and huge, ancient stone castle that sat way up high on its volcano perch, lording over the rest of the land while the surrounding town and suburbs sat quivering in its shadow, gazing up at its majestic power and beauty in great, stupendous awe.

I wanted to ask if we'd be going to Edinburgh someday soon. At school, before we were cruelly yanked away without even a say in the matter, there had been talk about a trip down to the old city for educational purposes, but that little adventure was well and truly off the table for the time being.

I wanted to ask if we could go there sometime. And I almost did. I wanted to know if dad was actually from there or had lived there at some point in his past, since he clearly spoke about the place with so much more fondness and pride than any of the other places he'd been to.

But it wasn't worth the risk to ask a question or to even interrupt him while he was off on one of his rants or singing along to one of his songs on the radio. Like I said, it was always hard to tell which direction his mood might swing. And if he thought it was a stupid question then, boy, oh boy, were you in trouble. And that's when memories of the last question I'd ever asked him pulsated through my mind, and a shiver ran up and down my spine with the painful memory of it all.

From that day forward, I'd learned my lesson to never bring up the subject of my mother again, or to ask any kind of burning questions that I may have, for that matter. So, I hope you can understand my reservations of questioning him in the future or even answering him back. No, not until I was old enough and smart enough to get the hell away from his clutches for good - not until that day would I ever provoke him or get on his bad side again. That was the plan.

I'd never been to a big city before, especially one as massive and as densely populated as Glasgow. I'd read about it in books and seen pictures of various sections of it at school. My dad didn't believe in televisions or computers or the internet. Devices of the devil, he'd always referred to them. Pointless objects that would have no use whatsoever when it came to survive after the apocalypse. So, we never really had access to any of them inside our home. Although, I'd bet everything I owned including my sanitary on him having access to all of them at his work.

But, I suppose, looking at pictures of something wasn't quite the same as actually being there, walking there, looking at the streets and buildings there, and watching the people, hearing the many different sounds, accents, and voices there while taking in all those various, new, wickedly wonderful scents and also the horrendous stinky ones.

When we drove into the heart of the city just an hour or so after the late sunset, I couldn't take my eyes away from the amazing, hypnotic lights. My sister too was in complete and utter awe at all the wonderful, different coloured lights and fast-moving cars and various people of all shapes, sizes, colour, and creed, all out on the streets as she glanced out through one window and I glanced out through the other.

"Dinnae let that shite oot there seduce ye girls, eh," dad casually chimed in, interrupting our new viewing pleasure and experience. "Aye, it aw looks pretty enuff fae the ootside, ah dare say. But looks can be deceiving in this world, ma girls. A lesson ye's are baeth aboot tae learn the night, as a matter of fact. Tonight, ah want ye's tae look beyond the lights. Beyond the glitz and the glamor. I want ye's tae see the sick, infested guts of this fuckin rat hole. The shite, scum, and bile that sits behind the seduction."

When I made a quick glance over at my dad, I caught his face in the rear-view mirror. The glint in his eyes and the devilish grin on his face, chilled me to the bone. I swiftly turned my attention back to the beautiful, hypnotic lights as we continued to drive even deeper into the heart of the city.

Dad parked on a little side street that overlooked a great big square surrounded by some grand old buildings. High upon one of those buildings, directly in front of us, towering over all the rest, I noticed a huge banner that seemed to beam out, projecting itself over the entire world.

The banner read 'People Make Glasgow.'

I kind of liked it. It made me smile. I could imagine living here and walking the streets and seeing that sign every time I glanced up and then feel proud that I was one of those good people who made the city what it was. Maybe I liked the thought of it because it went totally against every single word that my father had spoken throughout the entire four-hour journey south.

I was tempted to point the banner out to him, well at least point it out to my sister, but then I thought better of it. I didn't think either her or him would appreciate the words of that humble message. Then, like he had just read my mind, dad glanced up at the huge banner way up in the sky too. He smirked then gave out a loud, disgusting snort.

"'People make Glesgae. Ha. Ma fuckin arse they dae."

We watched for the next few hours as hundreds and hundreds of excitable people, mostly young men and women, passed by our parked car in the city centre. The ones in groups all looked so merry, particularly the women who were all dressed up so nice and sparkly and in different pretty shoes and beautiful tight-fitting dresses and skirts—skirts that my sister and I would never be allowed to wear in a million years because they seemed so short and revealing.

"Av goat fuckin belts that would dae a better job of hiding ma modesty than what they fuckin tramps are wearin," dad casually remarked.

Most of the beautiful and sparkly-dressed girls were singing in unison as they went on their merry way along the busy streets. The majority of whom I thought were even better singers than dad anyhow, but there was no way on this earth that I was ever going to tell him that.

When they weren't singing to each other, then those same young women and men were chatting loud, vibrantly and erratically, with each other like they were talking to someone on the other side of the street, even though they were only yards apart. None of them seemed to care less though whether the other people passing them by heard their volatile conversations or not.

What struck me the most was that they all just seemed so happy. Like they were having so much fun and really enjoying themselves. I'd never seen anything like it before. And I'd be lying if I didn't say that I got a wee bit caught up in the moment myself. In that instant I felt like running away from dad's car, running as fast as my little legs could carry me and join in with them. Join in with their fun and laughter and joy. Disappear into that vibrant

Glasgow nightlife with them forever. Never to return to my miserable life under my father's rule of thumb ever again.

But it was only a fleeting fantasy. No more, no less. I could never leave my sister in his manipulative, strong holding grasp. What would ever become of her if I abandoned her now? I shuddered at the thought. Though we had nothing else in this world, we had each other. We always had each other no matter what. Whatever happened in the future, at least, my father would never be able to take that away from us.

"Look at them. They aw pissed as fuckin farts," dad suddenly stated as if that explained the happy and merry peoples' crazy and boisterous behaviour from birth until that very moment. "They aw drunk on booze and drugs and fuck knows whit else shite they been shovelling intae their bodies. High as fuckin kites they are. Aye, at the start of the night and oan the surface, it aw looks like grand old fun and games, ye ken. But just gie it a few mare hoors for aw that shite in their veins tae wear off. Yul soon see the chaos and carnage it brings. Yul soon see their true colours then, ma girls."

We drove around some more. From the back seat, my sister and I continued to eagerly watch the brightly lit city come even more crazily to life as more and more excited and energetic bodies bounced and skipped around through the vibrant streets.

Dad then pulled up outside a late-night café and surprisingly took us both inside for a late-night meal. This was something most unexpected and something that dad never did. He didn't believe in having other people cook meals for you or having big chain stores like Asda, Tesco, and Sainsburys to supply you with all their contaminated processed foods. He only believed in growing your own, hunting your own. What you catch and kill, you eat and make good of. Nothing else. Hence, we only ever enjoyed junk food when we were out on our own little adventures, stealing and acquiring it for ourselves from the unlucky campers and tourists who crossed our path.

But dad said it was our special treat for surviving out in the forest for three days and three nights, all by ourselves and for the first time of asking too. He said we could choose anything on the menu, anything at all. So, we both chose a cheeseburger and strawberry milkshake (my sister had chocolate) and a side of fries.

We'd never been allowed anything like this before in our lives, so we were both a little cautious at first that it might be some kind of test. Some dirty trick that as soon as we decided what we'd like to eat from the menu, dad would swiftly grab us both by the roots of the hair and drag us the hell out of there, back to the car. Back up the long road leading home. Another test failed. But he didn't. In fact, he overly insisted and even bought a single sloppy bacon burger for himself too just to prove to us how serious he was. However, once we'd sat down at a free table and finally ordered, did the twist finally reveal itself.

"Make the maist of this, ma girls. Cuz, it'll never fuckin happen again. Not while yur baeth sure as shite living under ma roof, that's for fuckin sure."

When the waitress brought the food over, me and my sister swiftly tucked into the goods immediately, devouring our tasty, salty meals almost as quickly as they'd been placed in front of us. I was eating so fast because I couldn't believe our luck. For me, the quicker we ate the less chance there'd be for dad to change his mind and slap our plates away from underneath our noses, right off the table, just as soon as his mood changed.

But all he did the entire time was chuckle at our eagerness. It was the first time I'd ever seen him so laid back and almost, well, almost so normal and nice. He was unrecognizable, in fact. For a brief, heartfelt moment, I thought that it might be a small sign of some good, positive changes to come. That this was what it felt like to be part of a proper, normal family. To sit down and enjoy a meal with your loved ones without fear of disappointment.

Turned out though I was very wrong.

Once dad had finished his burger, he grabbed one of the late-night café newspapers lying in a nearby rack for customers to help themselves to. He opened the thick tabloid and started to read.

"Let's see whit rancid shite am missing oot on in the world the day then, eh," he said with a sinister scoff and so excruciatingly loud that everybody inside the half-full café could hear.

"Whit a fuckin load of pish!" he cried as he flicked through all the colourful tabloid gossip stories, before unexpectedly throwing the paper in disgust at a young couple sitting at the table beside us. It almost knocked over the girl's milkshake, but neither of the two said a single word in protest once they caught a glance of the evil, sadistic snarl coming from dad's face.

"Fuck ye's looking at?"

The couple quickly went back to minding their own business. Dad turned back to us and immediately went into one of his rants, full throttle this time, like nothing I'd ever heard from him before, unless he was talking about his beloved apocalypse.

"...That's the fuckin problem wi people in this cuntree the day, ken. They're aw media driven, zombified, tabloid fuckin junky bastards. It's their bible, ken. Tabloid newspapers are bibles for the working and lower-class people of this new shitey Britain of the twenty-first century."

"If there's something in they horse-shite, slanderous, no-even-gid-tae-wipe-your-ain-backside papers, aboot some celebrity fuckwit fae the X factor sleepin aroond wi some married TV slut, host, whore, or some bloody, premiere-league fitbaw player, snorting a tram line of coke while shagging his way through the spice girls, then it just hus tae be the anly important fuckin thing going oan in the world right noo, aeh? Nuttin else seems tae matter a fuck tae these cunts! Oh, so David and Natasha huv been voted auf Britain's got fuck aw talent, aye. Superb! But in other, less significant news, two hundred thousand brown people died in a massive earthquake oan the other side of the fuckin planet. Oh well. Nay luck. Back tae Dermot oan fuckin 'strictly cum aw over ma fuckin chebs, dancing,' ye bastard. If it's no news aboot rich, white, western celebrity-folk then we dinnae wantae fucking ken aboot it, dae we?"

My dad finally paused for breath. His eyes were glazed with a burning, psychotic rage. He took a long sip from his big glass of orange juice, gulping it down almost to its completion, before slamming the near empty glass back down on the table with a frightening vigour.

My sister was smiling wildly and avidly listening to my father's every word. She was enjoying the show immensely. I, on the other hand, was very nervous and uncomfortable. I could see most of the eyes and the expressions from the café's paying customers seated all around us, all of them were solely focused on our table—my raving lunatic father, in particular.

I glanced over at the chefs and waitresses too, all of them anxiously chatting away about which one of them should come over and tell the crazy man with the kids to shut up or leave. Whatever was going to go down next, I didn't like the feeling I was getting in the pit of my stomach about what might happen if one of these nice, innocent folks did come over and say something on behalf of everyone else who just wanted to have a quiet meal and chat amongst themselves.

"We live in a world where thousands of people die every single fuckin day fae serious fucking shite. Thousands mare are badly injured whilst brave, hardworking others are helping those less fortunate get back oan tae their fuckin feet again. Noo if that's no real fuckin news then ah dinnae ken wit fuckin is."

"Ye ken, ah could safely say that oot of aw the peeps in this fuckin cuntree, ninety nine percent of they clueless bastards are utterly fuckin mind-warped by aw they tabloid/media cunts. Maybe mare so in the elderly likes cuz, let's face it, they auld bastards have even less tae dae wi their time than the rest of us 'up tae oor eyeballs in debt' bastards."

I watched as an old couple at the back of the café just shook their heads and tutted dad's remarks, but again they didn't pipe up and say a single word in my father's direction. Like everyone else there they just sat back and took it, trying their best to ignore the crazy man and get on with whatever it was they were pretending to do.

"And dinnae get me sterted oan aw they bludy numpty, clueless, talk show hosts either. Some of they slanderous cunty bawed, shite bag, bastards would have ye convinced that they're the ones actually running this cuntree, ken. And that their uneducated opinions matter a flying fuck tae the rest of us. Which they dinnae of course. No for one smelly ginger baw-haired second dae they fucking matter. Anly tae cunts wi a TV who dinnae have a bawbag clue wit tae dae wi their precious time on this planet, does that shite fuckin matter."

Dad paused for breath. This time though he sat right back against the comfy booth chair. He looked so smug and proud and was grinning wildly. Like he owned this audience all around the cafe. Like his words actually mattered to these people's good normal lives when all they truly wanted was him to shut the hell up and go away.

"But who knows, aye?" dad continued, shrugging his shoulders for effect. "Maybe there are good people oot there who really dinnae gie a shiten hoot and nanny aboot anything the media shoves intae oor faces. People who can just turn their backs oan it aw and throw their fuckin TVs, phones, and computers right oot the fuckin windae and say, *Ye ken wit baw-jaws! Ah really dinnae gee a fuck. Ah really dinnae gee a flying fuck, ye fannies, aboot anyhin ye have tae say in yer shitey trashy tabloids and tv shows. Cuz ah have ma ain unpolluted brain and ma ain unpolluted opinions.* Just like us, aeh girls? Just like us."

He winked at both me and my sister, but I could tell it was more for my sister, who, by the look of things and by the way she was leaning over the table, all doe-eyed, was ready to eat out of the palm of his hand.

"The media tells us wit tae eat. Wit tae drink. Wit tae buy and how tae live oor fuckin lives. Where does it bludy well aw end likes, ken?"

Dad hesitated again. He looked down towards his feet with a look of great sorrow, shaking his head with a bitter disgust. After a few, long, anxious and awkward seconds he quickly glanced back up at us, his main audience in this arena, as if suddenly remembering something else to rant on about. Something else that his audience might want to hear—no, in fact, *needed* to hear until our ear drums burst and our lobes bled red.

"And dinnae even get me started oan independence, ye cunts."

Dad took a long hard look around the entire room after he said that. I couldn't believe that he was trying to look every single person in the café directly in the eye, but not even one of them was able to meet his stare.

"But ken whit: aw ye cunts are in for one big fuckin surprise soon enuf, because it's coming. This big fucking thing that's gonnae change everything. And ah mean EVERYTHING! Well, it's coming. It's oan its way. And nane of ye's. Nane of you's baw-jawed bastards are even ready for it."

Dad then spat on the floor with sheer disgust. Still, nobody said a word. Finally, he stopped ranting and raving. The whole entire café didn't know which way to turn and neither did I for that matter. Then my sister started clapping like some over-enthusiastic seal. Again, I didn't know which way to look; I felt so embarrassed. Like I wanted a big dark hole underneath the table to open up and swallow every single person there whole, all except for me and my sister.

I didn't know how or even why, perhaps it was that sharp look-of-daggers scowl on my father's face when he glanced at me next, but I eventually started clapping too. Just to keep on his good side.

He made a move to leave.

"Mon then girls. Let's get the fuck oot of this polluted shitehole."

My sister was still so excited that as she stood up, she even had the audacity to ask dad if she could have another milkshake, even if just to take away with her.

"Do ah look like a fuckin piggy bank, eh?" dad replied. His foul mood reigning over us again like the return of a familiar storm slowly rolling its way over the mountain tops beside us. And without even looking back at the eyes of pity which fell upon both my sister and I, all three of us left the café.

Chapter 9

It was getting late. Really late. Dad was still driving around the vibrant city centre, mumbling to himself every so often about something that I couldn't quite make out. When he did say something that was just barely audible for me to hear it was more or less along the lines of: 'These people are a fuckin disease and we are the fuckin cure.'

At first, I didn't have a clue what he was looking for that night as he patrolled the streets of Glasgow, cruising from one grubby wee side street to the next, or of what actions he might partake in, if any. All that I knew was that I desperately wanted to fall into a deep and blissful sleep after eating all that sugary, fatty food. But even more than that, I just wished to go home.

Suddenly, dad pulled the car over onto a curb halfway down a little street that ran adjacent to a huge, towering railway station. With sleepy but curious eyes, my sister and I glanced at each other for a brief moment yet none of us said a word. Then it soon became abundantly clear, very quickly in fact, as to why dad had stopped on this particular street when a very bold and attractive woman, wearing ripped black stockings, a tight black mini skirt, and an even tighter cropped white top, approached the driver's side window like she knew dad or, at the very least, had no fear of him whatsoever. Instantly, I found myself loving her confidence. I secretly wished that I could be as bold and as confident as her one day, or even to just walk around with that same fearless swagger. Apart from my father, It was something that I'd only ever seen in my sister before.

"You looking for business sweetheart, aye?" the woman casually stated. For the life of me I couldn't think what business dad could possibly have with such an empowering woman.

"Aye," dad swiftly replied with a glint in his eye and cheerful snort. "Ye any good at plumbing likes?"

"Av been aroond a few pipes in ma time, sweetheart. Ah think ah can manage getting ma hands aroond yours," the woman replied with a sly wink and without missing a beat. Like she'd had this very same conversation a thousand and one times before. Their strange, almost forced, crypted chat, absolutely baffled me though.

"Good girl. Jump in then, Hen."

When she climbed into the passenger seat, I noticed a rake load of scars and marks all over her arms and wrists. She had a faded scar too about four inches in length across her cheek, on the left side of her face. Even up close I still thought she was beautiful though, in a raw, earthly kind of way, and those scars just gave her so much more character, made her so much more interesting to look at.

Of course, I wanted to ask how she'd gotten such wounds on her body. Perhaps she'd enjoyed living out in the wilderness too from time to time, trying to survive with nothing but her wits and her own two hands to aid her, but I didn't dare say a thing. Not while dad was sitting right beside her. Only when he drove away did the woman finally notice my sister and I sitting in the cloaked darkness of the back seats, right behind her.

"Whit the fuck are they daen back there?" said the woman aghast. The woman who'd looked like she'd seen it all. Her cool and confident persona evaporated in seconds.

"Dinnae ye worry aboot them. They're just ma bairns, that's aw."

"Jesus Christ. Am no daen ye wi fuckin minors in the back. Are ye sick in the heed?"

"Dinnae be silly, woman. What kind of man dae ye think ah am, eh? Ramming ye in front of ma ain bairns? Are ye auf yer fuckin rocker?"

The woman continued to look utterly freaked out. Whatever business with dad she had in mind, it was clearly something that my sister and I weren't clearly meant to be a part of.

"It's no right this. Av goat kids of ma ain tae and they dinnae even know whit ah dae tae make ends meet. Naw. This isnae right. Jist let me oot at the end of the street, pal, and we'll say nay mare aboot it, aye?"

We were driving along, past a vast black river now. Dad quickly shoved his hand into his pockets and pulled out a large wad of cash notes. I think they were twenty-pound ones. He crammed them down between the woman's thighs which I thought was a little improper to touch someone down there, but the woman didn't seem to mind at all.

"Half noo. Half efter," dad bluntly stated.

The woman hesitated. She glanced away from me and my sister and pulled out the money from between her legs. She looked at the crumpled notes for a long time. Like they were the answer to all her prayers. They seemed to hypnotise her into submission though. Finally, she let out a deep, defeated sigh and her whole, tense body seemed to relax.

"Awright. But naw anywhere near the car, awright. The Bairns dinnae get tae see, aye?"

A look of bitter disgust wafted across dad's face.

"What kind of sicko freak dae ye think ah um, eh? Ye dinnae even ken what ah want ye tae dae yet, fucks sake."

"Aye, well, if your like every other man av ever met in ma puff, then I cannae see there being tae many surprises there, sweetheart."

The further we travelled along the wide black river, the darker the city became. Like my sister, I had no idea what we were doing or even where the hell we were going. For a second, I even considered that this woman might be our own mother. Ridiculous as that thought may have seemed at the time - that she'd been away from us for such a long period of time that she'd somehow forgotten who she really was and who we actually were. But I quickly shook that notion out of my mind. She looked nothing like me or my sister. And without the scars she seemed far too young to be a mother to anyone our age, but then again, she had stated that she did have kids of her own back at home. Boy, they had to be young though.

"Where we going anyhoo?" the woman asked. "Ah know a good wee spot if ye jist turn aroond here and go back tae that red building back there likes, sweetheart."

"Ah ken a better spot," dad firmly replied, and within thirty seconds he was slowing down and pulling in beside an old and abandoned, half-demolished factory. He then took a slow, right hand turn just past the broken factory brick walls and drove into a dark, narrow and secluded alleyway.

"Well, ye learn sumthin new every day, aye? Am fae Glesgae and ah didnae even know this place existed."

Dad drove all the way to the end of the alley. The lights of the car lit up the blood-red brick walls on either side of us before beaming hard off the old brick wall at the end as we approached. Dad stopped the car. He turned off the engine followed by the headlights. Darkness swarmed over us in seconds like a black plague.

"Right," said the woman, turning back to face us in the pitch black. "You guys stay here and behave yourselves, aye. Me and yur da are jist nippin oot tae the other side uv the alley tae dae a wee bit uv business. It shouldnae take very…"

Like a flash of thunder and lightning exploding from the darkness, dad started punching and pounding the woman with his bare fists. He must have punched her a dozen or so times, over and over again in the nose and mouth, before he finally stopped. I was too shocked and scared to even move a muscle. I felt wet, warm liquid splattering all over my face too with every crunch of his knuckles on the poor woman's face.

I couldn't see a damn thing though. Only dark flashes of aggressive shadows followed by flickers of even faster shadows. But I could hear every excruciating, gruelling sound of what was happening in those front two seats.

When dad finally stopped pounding the woman's face, he took a deep breath and relaxed. I could hear the woman making some kind of low-pitched yelp. She wasn't screaming, shouting, or saying anything, just making that strange, eerie shuddering yelp and wheeze, which could have been coming from her nose rather than her mouth.

Dad turned on the headlights again. He opened his driver's door and climbed out of the car. For the first time, I got a good, proper look at what my father had done to that nice, friendly, confident, and attractive, if not a little too talkative, woman.

She lay sprawled out, half conscious in the passenger seat. Her shoulder-length, dirty blonde hair was now a mop of sticky red ooze. Same as her face. Most of the blood seemed to be coming from her flattened nose. Her mouth and jaw looked a little off-centre. She seemed to be trying to open her mouth every now and again like some kind of broken robot, but only her lips seemed to move, just a little. She reminded me of one of the fishes that my sister had recently caught back at the loch where we stayed, lying utterly helpless in our hands as it pouted its lips in and out, up and down, desperately trying to breathe.

She was breathing though. Her chest was lifting up and down, deep and slow, while little bubbles of blood, spit, and mucus throbbed around her nose. Dad opened the passenger side door and pulled the woman out of the car. As he dragged her in front of the bonnet, he told me and my sister to get the hell out and follow him.

I hesitated at first, but my sister had a wild look in her eyes. She already had her hand on the door handle, eagerly waiting to get a closer look at what my father was going to do next. She opened the door and stepped outside. I reluctantly followed. What else could I do? I had to go with them. Dad sat the woman down against the back-brick wall of the alleyway, right in front of the strong car headlights. She looked extremely horrific, unrecognizable in fact from when we'd picked her up off the street only a few minutes earlier. Blood continued to pour out from her nose, drenching its way through her clothes and upper body.

"Puulease…. Wu…why…" I heard her finally whine through her broken jaw. Or at least that's what I thought I'd heard her say. She was mumbling her words, unable to open her mouth and form proper sentences.

My sister and I approached the front of the car. My dad came towards us. He sat down on the bonnet beside us, looking all smug and casual like.

"You remembered to bring your fuckin knives, aye? Like ah told ye's tae, aye?"

Without taking her eyes away from the bleeding, injured woman, my sister gently nodded. In that moment I felt the blood flowing in my veins swiftly turn to ice. I couldn't take another step forward. I couldn't speak. I couldn't even think. I knew what he wanted us to do and I felt sick to my guts.

"Noo finish her. Anyway, ye's want. Stab the bitch. Slit her fuckin throat. Whitever takes yur fancy."

My sister darted a glance over at me. Her eyes were wide and filled with both danger and excitement, but she also seemed a little scared too, just a wee hint of fear that I only I caught a glimpse of, so you could've imagined how I was feeling.

I'd never seen fear like that before in my sister's demeanour. She was usually so calm and collected in these situations. Well, when the killing of animals was involved, she had no remorse or fear whatsoever. She just did it. She enjoyed doing it, she'd done it so often. But this was different. This was a whole, entirely different beast all together. This was another living person. Another human being. Just like us. Just like her.

"Dinnae look at yur fuckin sister. And dinnae even fuckin hesitate either. Just get over there the pair of ye's and fuckin dae whit ye's are telt."

My sister turned back to the woman. As she approached, she pulled out her hunting knife that had been tucked up inside her belt. The woman, still dazed, confused, and bleeding, was gradually becoming more and more alert by the second. Again, she tried to speak and cry out from behind her broken face.

"Puulease… Naw…. Pulllease… dinnae."

Beside me, dad just sneered and impatiently folded his arms. I watched my sister move even closer towards the woman who tried to back away, further against the wall, but all she ended up doing was moving sideways, moving along the bricks and into the tight corner of the alley.

I remained frozen with fear and just stood there watching my sister move ever closer towards the woman. She was stalking up on her like she was some wounded deer that needed to be finished off so that we could eat that night and survive.

In that terrifying moment I prayed that dad wouldn't notice me still standing there paralysed, doing absolutely nothing. Praying that he wouldn't tell me to take out my knife too and get over there to join my sister. But then the inevitable happened, he turned towards me and kicked my thigh, nudging me forward a few steps.

"On ye go then. Go join your fuckin sister."

I don't know how, but I found myself moving forward. I found myself walking up to stand beside my sister, but it wasn't me controlling those steps. I felt like I was on some kind of autopilot. Like it was someone else, some higher force making those movements for me. I didn't understand what was happening anymore. The best way to describe it was like some out-of-body experience. Was I even here? I wondered over and over again, expecting to wake up from that brutal nightmare at any given second and find myself sprawled out on top of my sister in the back of our car as my father continued to drive along the never-ending road north, back to our home.

But I didn't wake up from that nightmare.

My sister stood over the woman. Arms spread wide. Knife clenched hard in her hand. Ready to strike. The sharp blade glistening in the headlights. The woman tried her utmost to get back up onto her knees but her arms soon gave way. She just didn't have the strength and balance to even crawl anymore. She began sobbing and breathing hard as if she was going to hyperventilate.

"Puu-lease. Why... why are ye's... daen this...? Pu-lease"

My sister stepped closer. She clenched her knife even harder. I really believed that she was going to stab the woman and soon. I knew it in my heart. She would never go against dad. Never. Like night would always follow day, my sister was guaranteed do anything that my father asked of her. She lived and breathed for his pride. For his respect.

"Just one stab at a time, mind," came dad's chilling voice. "You, then yur sister, then back again. Make sure ye's baeth get a good wee shot while she's still alive. Ah want ye's tae baeth get a good feel of what it's like tae take a life."

I could see my sister's breathing becoming harder and faster, just like the woman's, like she was building herself up to make her strike like some kind of wild queen cobra. She even started grunting and groaning out through her gritted teeth like a car accelerator, revving herself up more and more, readying to accelerate into her target. I'd never heard such a sound come out of my sister's mouth before. It horrified me to my core.

"Hurry the fuck up," dad continued. "We've no got aw night here, ken?"

The woman raised her hands as far as they would go, as if to protect herself from the brutal slices, stabs, and slashes that were about to severely unleash upon her.

"Noooooo…. Puleaseeeeaaaa Nooooo," the woman painfully yelled and sobbed.

Suddenly, I threw up. I didn't even notice it was happening at first. The nausea came over me so fast. Everything I'd eaten in the past twenty-four hours came out of me all at once.

I heard my sister drop her knife. Relieved of the distraction, she stepped away from the woman and rushed over to comfort me and to see if I was okay.

"For fuck's sake!" I heard dad yell.

I fell onto my knees and vomited again. My sister crouched down beside me. She started rubbing and patting my back. At the same time, I heard dad get off the car bonnet. He came storming over towards us in a blaze of fury. Shaking his head, he kicked me hard down onto the floor so that I landed right in my own sick, then he pulled my sister back up onto her feet.

"Ah expected that kind of cowardly shite fae her, but no fae you. No fae fuckin you."

Dad dragged my sister back over towards the woman. He picked up my sister's knife and shoved the handle back into her hand.

"NOO FUCKIN STAB THE BITCH!" he roared.

My sister started shaking her head. For the first time since I could remember, tears began streaming down her face.

"FUCKIN STAB HER YE STUPID WEE CUNT. STAB HER. FUCKIN STAB HER!"

My sister dropped her knife again. She began crying hysterically that she couldn't. That she just couldn't.

Raging, my dad threw my sister ferociously against the side alley wall. She smacked her head hard and fell to the ground, still very conscious. The woman was sobbing out even harder. Still begging for her life. Pleading and mumbling something about her own children. She knew the end was nigh. We all did. It was only a matter of time unless there was some kind of miraculous intervention from the outside world.

In a rage of pure and utter, frustrated insanity, dad picked up my sister's knife with his right hand. With his left he grabbed the woman by the roots of her dirty blonde, blood-stained hair and lifted her right up off the ground with a freakish strength. Like he'd done to me once before in the past when I'd asked that stupid question about my mother, but this was a fully-grown woman.

He then began stabbing her all over her upper body, all over her face, neck, throat, chest, arms, breasts, repeatedly, over and over, until she was just a mop of silent and unrecognizable, blood, pulp, and flesh.

As my father continued to stab the poor, defenceless woman again and again, I somehow began to see my mother's face in her, even though I had no recollection of what my mother even looked like, since I'd never even seen a picture of her before. And in that one, crazy, surreal, horrific but sadistically beautiful moment, I finally realized what fate had befallen our own mother.

"Ye want something done right, then dae it yur fuckin self. That's whit ma da always used tae say," raged dad once he'd finally finished stabbing. He was still clinging onto the roots of the dead woman's hair and didn't look like he'd be letting go anytime soon.

Both my sister and I were still on the ground. Her, sitting up against the side wall; me, still lying flat on my stomach and face soaked in my own vomit. "Am only trying tae teach ye's something here, ma girls," dad continued with a gentler, unfamiliar tone. "Give ye's a life lesson here for fucks sake. Give ye's some kind of practice and experience for the future for when ye's huv tae really dae something like this wi-oot even thinking aboot it. So that ye's can one day save your ain lives. Kill or be killed."

Over beside the alley wall, my sister wiped away her tears.

"Dinnae shed tears for this. Ye dinnae shed tears for aw they deer, fish, rabbits, and squirrels you've killed and butchered over the years. Believe me, they're much worthier of life than this fuckin pathetic thing lying here. This thing is just one part of the problem why this world is gonna, one day, very fuckin soon, implode in oan itself. Scum like her and aw they other walking deadbeat trash you saw oot there on they city streets the night. None of them are worthy of your fuckin tears or your fuckin pity. So, the sooner ye's get that through yer thick fuckin heeds, the better auf your baeth gonna be in this life."

Dad hesitated. He took a few deep breaths. He was trying to regain his composure. The look on his face at that precise moment told me that he was in pain. An emotional pain of turmoil.

"Am actually, truly fuckin hurt the noo, ma girls. Ah thought ad brought ye's up stronger than this. More bold and brave. More savy and street smart. Yuv really fuckin hurt ma feelings the night girls. Truly. Av never been so embarrassed or ashamed of ma ain fuckin kin before. Never. Never in ma whole entire life than ah am at this very moment in time."

He ranted some more about how we both still weren't ready. That we needed so much more training and exercises to make us harder, stronger, and sterner inside. We needed a cold, hard, ruthless streak he said. And more important than anything else, we needed our emotions—pity and remorse—thoroughly gutted from the inside out.

Chapter 10

I didn't want to fall asleep, even though I was more tired than I'd ever been before in my life. I did everything I could within my power to desperately clutch to consciousness, but I felt too emotionally drained after everything that had happened that night. And within one hour of dad driving back up north again, I'd joined my sister in the black world of deep sleep as we huddled together on the back seat.

After dad had killed that woman, he'd swiftly ushered us back inside the car as he proceeded to wrap her soulless, lifeless, bloodied body up in a dozen black bin liners. Next, he taped them all together until not a single drop of her blood or foul, rotting odour could seep its way out through the bin bags.

With my heart still pumping at the back of my throat, I watched him lift the mummified body up onto his shoulders before throwing it into the boot of our car. At first, I thought he was just going to dump the poor woman's remains into that wide, black river that flowed west on the opposite side of the alleyway to us. But when he began driving into the night without stopping, eventually taking the A road back up north again, just as the new dawn was beginning to gently break into the darkness of the east, I quickly realised that he had something else in store for us.

When I woke up it was bright daylight outside. The sun was shining in from the passenger window on my left, which meant that it was sitting high up in the north west and gradually making its decline back down to the horizon again. My heart skipped a beat as I quickly realised that the time of day was well into the late afternoon. I'd slept nonstop for roughly eight or nine hours. What also didn't make sense was the fact that the car was very stationary, yet I could still feel a gentle rocking motion from side to side. Then there was that strange, see-through roof, directly above our car and two huge white walls on either side.

I sat up. There was no one in the vehicle but me. When I took my first proper glance out through the car window, I could see another half a dozen or so cars all parked around ours, either side of the huge white walls. But to my rear, all I could see was water. The cold, hard, rough, grey water of the sea.

Another series of shivers ran down my spine. I must be on a ship. There was no other explanation for it. In front of me, north by north west, where the sun was towering overhead, must've been the front of the ship. It was some kind of small, open-topped ferry but I still couldn't make head nor tails of it all.

I'd seen plenty of ships before, big and small, sailing past our farm house on the coast from time to time, but I'd never actually been on one until that very moment. I felt a little anxious but excited at the same time. Where the hell was I? And where was my father? Most importantly of all, where the hell was my bloody sister?

The car was unlocked. I opened the door and climbed outside. I made my way towards the nearest barrier railings on the other side of the huge white walls. I couldn't see any other people around, so I just stood still for a while, gripping the railing hard while I glanced hypnotically down at the trailing grey water beneath.

When I glanced back, following the white wavy tracks of the ferry, I could see the faint sign of a distant land way over on the south-eastern horizon. That must be Scotland. That must've been where we boarded the ship.

Turning my head and glancing towards the front of the ferry, I couldn't see any land at all. Just acres and acres of dull grey sea. For a fleeting second a funny wee thought entered my mind - even with sunshine and blue skies in Scotland, the sea still remained a miserable, dull grey.

I made my way over towards the front of the ship, before pushing my way through a strong steel door and heading up some inside steps towards the upper decks. A family of five passed me by on their way down. Most of them smiled at me, while I did not. More people came into my view. A group of middle-aged tourists with cameras. I say tourists because they looked nothing like the Scottish people I knew. They had darker, healthier-looking skin for a start, unlike the sickly pale white of most Scottish folks I'd been in contact with throughout my life. They all had nice smiles though and sparkling happy eyes that made me slightly jealous and suspicious of them.

Out on this new deck I instantly spotted my father and sister. They sat together at the very front of the outdoor seating area. Dad, wearing a dark pair of sunglasses, had his feet firmly up upon the rails and seemed to be sleeping soundly. My sister had her feet up too but looked wide awake. She seemed to be just gazing out at the endless sea in front of her. Hypnotically deep in thought.

She looked so beautiful, peaceful and innocent in that moment, like all little girls should look at our age. Trouble free with no worries and not a care in the world. But Jesus, how looks can be so deceiving. Especially that of a preteen girl. To look at us both right then, no one would've been able to guess in a million years all the cruel horrors and hardships we'd been forced to endure, and not just last night, but for the entirety of our young lives together.

Without making a sound, I sat gently down beside my sister. She turned and smiled warmly at me before taking my hand in hers. She asked if I wanted to go for a wander around the ship. There was a café down below where we could get some food and drink. I was hungry, so it sounded like a good idea.

We both gazed up at dad who was snoring away for Scotland. My sister smiled and giggled at his antics. I did not. I couldn't even force a fake cheerful laugh in that moment if my life depended on it. I wanted nothing more than to get away from his presence before he had the chance to wake up and rant and rave some more about our failures from the night before and how disappointed he still was with us both, especially me.

Hand in hand, my sister led us down to the surprisingly quiet café way down on the lower deck. I felt absolutely famished, and was now looking forward to eating something, anything. I chose a cheese and ham sandwich and a glass of orange juice while my sister just had an orange juice. She paid with some change dad had given her earlier.

We sat down a few tables along from an old couple who smiled at us with big gooey eyes like my sister and I were their long-lost grandchildren. We didn't smile back though and tried our best to ignore them and discourage them from doing anything else but look.

As I ate my sandwich, I urgently wanted to ask my sister her thoughts and feelings about what had happened the night before back in Glasgow. Thoughts that I furiously battled to believe were even true and perhaps weren't just a bad nightmare I'd had while sleeping all day in the car, which I secretly knew, deep down inside, was not the case. But I just couldn't bring myself to say anything to my sister. I knew she wouldn't like it and I knew she wouldn't want to speak about it either, especially after breaking down in a fit of uncontrollable sobs and not being able to go through with my father's wishes, which was not like her at all.

Instead, I asked why we were on the ferry and where exactly we were supposed to be going. Surely, we should have been home hours ago. She told me that she'd woken up shortly before they'd boarded the ferry at Ullapool. I'd heard of Ullapool. I'd never been there before, but it was almost the same distance North from our home as Glasgow was South from it.

I asked her why we'd travelled so far north. My sister just shrugged her shoulders and said that dad was taking us someplace special for another test. That he was still deeply upset and felt let down by us after what had happened last night. But he hadn't yet spoken to her about what this so-called test might be about. All she knew was that we were heading over to one of the remotest and furthest north-easterly islands of Scotland—The isle of Lewis. And whatever happened once we got there was anyone's guess.

I prayed to anyone who might listen—to any of the hundred and one gods up there in the skies and space that we wouldn't have to try and kill some nice and innocent young woman again. I really prayed hard about that.

Chapter 11

We were on the ferry for around two and a half hours before we finally came into a small-town port on the new coast.

Dad was fully awake and surprisingly seemed in very good spirits. He made no mention of the night before either, as he ushered us to sit beside him at the front of the quiet ferry. He made us both watch, with a childlike glee, as the ferry came into port at Stornoway town, the capital of the Scottish Island. It was like we had never even left the main land in the first place. Still so much vibrant green and roaming hills, valleys, and lochs every which way you looked.

Back in the car Dad put on his radio again and, with his sunglasses still firmly transfixed to his face, began singing along to his tunes.

Within an hour, we had driven out to a distant, secluded clifftop somewhere in the north of the island. There, dad took out the body of the woman, still wrapped up in bin liners in the back of the car. He flung her over his shoulder before walking towards the edge of the cliff. He then lowered her body down into his arms, held her out in mid-air for a moment before letting her fall effortlessly into the rough sea and jagged rocks below.

"That's task numero uno oot the way," he bellowed in a cheerful jest. "Noo, ontae you guys," he continued with a sly glance straight at my sister and I.

"Noo, am taking ye's tae a very a special place. A special place very dear tae ma heart. A place where ma ain father once took me once upon a time. Although, ah was a wee bit mare older than ye guys are likes. But there's two of ye, aeh, so that should mare than make up for it."

I was still baffled to what the hell he was talking about and what was going to happen next, but nonetheless my curiosity had peaked. Whatever it was, I had to go along with or else face more of my father's infuriating wrath.

The sun finally set, and after driving along the island coast from north to northwest for another half an hour, dad pulled over onto the side of a narrow road. He exited the car and told us to get out too and follow him, which we did with no questions asked.

He led us along a rough, grassy terrain then finally up onto a small rocky hill that breathtakingly overlooked a series of huge and spacious standing stones that spiralled out this way and that upon a large distant plane. Even though the sun had fully set, there was still a good chunk of daylight lingering around in the western sky, so the strange-looking standing stones were still easily the focus of the surrounding valleys and hills.

"Behold the Standing Stanes of Callanish," dad cried as he sat himself down upon a small cluster of rocks on top of the hill. "Ma ain faither used tae bring me up here every noo and again," he continued before trailing off into silence.

I marvelled at the stones. The bigger ones seemed to be standing in a circle in the middle of the plane, while the largest of them stood all by itself right in the very centre. Another five rows of smaller, trailing stones took off from the centre and spread out in various directions.

I wanted to ask about them. *Why were they all standing upright like that? Who had put them there and arranged them all to stand up in such a way?* But the painful memories of asking him questions completely overwhelmed my pleasure for an answer. So instead I said nothing at all.

My sister though must have been reading my thoughts as she was the one who finally asked him a question regarding why the stones were unnaturally standing up the way they were?

"Becuz, ma girl, a tribe of silly cunts, a long, long time ago, thought they'd be a bunch of right smart-arses and stick them stanes in the groond for nay good reason whitsoever, just cuz they thought they were being funny bastards at the time, imagining all they baffled folk in the future, like us, raking their fuckin brains trying tae come up wi all these fancy, scientific, smart-arse answers why the ancient, silly cunts had arranged the stanes like that in the first place. Pure dead brilliant, aye?"

My sister just smiled and agreed. I, on the other hand, was not overly convinced of my father's explanation. It would have taken a great amount of time, care and effort and planning to arrange those magnificent big stones in such a way like that, and I'm pretty sure that thousands of years ago, time, along with the average human lifespan, would have been very precious indeed, preciously shorter than it was now, especially when they put in so much hard work and dedication into something that meant absolutely nothing.

"Ma faither used tae say though that it were an army of men who came tae overthrow a clan of mystical druids on the island and that it wis their magic which turned that same army intae stane. The same standing stanes ye's see before ye's noo."

Well that sounded a bit more plausible than his first story. But I didn't believe in magic and fairy tales and special powers, so I guess I'd just have to do more research on the matter myself. If I ever got to see a computer or the town library again. But none of his explanations so far addressed the reason to why he'd stated that the stones were a special place to him.

"Anyhoo," dad suddenly said as he suddenly stood back up onto his feet. "It really doesnae matter ah hoot who put they big fuckin stanes there or why they even put them there."

He then hesitated for a second and clapped his hands together, looking us both dead in the eye.

"What matters, girls, is that this place is the starting point of your next adventure. Fae here on in ah want ye's baeth tae make yur way back hame and by any means necessary and wi-oot drawing any attention tae yourselves in the slightest…"

At first, my heart absolutely sank to the pit of my stomach at his words. He was going to leave us out here in the middle of nowhere to fend for ourselves as we made our way back home again over hundreds and hundreds of miles without anyone's help, all for the sake of his silly wee games and to prove to him that we weren't children anymore.

But then the more his words settled into me, the more I realised that time without my father around and breathing down our necks was time that I valued greatly – in fact time that I deeply valued more than anything in the world these days.

"Nay time limit likes," he quickly added like he were doing us a huge favour. "And nay pressure. Obviously, the quicker ye's dae it the mare al be impressed. Ah think it took me just over a week the first-time ma auld man left me oot here…" a wry smile broadened across his face as he spoke his next sentence. "…but, by the fifth-time of asking ah wis a fuckin natural at it. Christ, ah was awmaist hame before him on mare than one occasion."

I gave out a questioning gaze to my sister. Already the sky was becoming black and the temperature was gradually dropping. My sister returned my gaze with warm, smiling eyes. I knew she'd be loving this. Any chance she could get to redeem and prove herself in front of my father, she would welcome with wide open arms.

Then, just like that, Dad started walking away.

"Well, good luck, ma girls. See's ye's baeth when ah see ye, ah guess. And dinnae get fuckin picked up by any police either or any kind of authority figures for that matter, or ah will be mightily pissed auf."

We both just stood there in silence as we watched our father stroll casually away, back towards his warm, comfortable, waiting car in the distance. We kept watching too, like little abandoned puppies, as he climbed inside, started his engine, beeped his horn, and waved back at us before driving carefully off, back up the rough single-track road from where we'd came.

For a few seconds, I thought that he might turn around and drive back for us with a big beaming smile on his face, while crying out *gotcha*, or *the jokes on you's' ye wee bastards. Look at both your wee faces. Noo get into the fuckin car.* But if you knew my father, then you knew that was never ever going to be a reliable outcome.

When the lights of his car finally disappeared over the distant hills and horizon, my sister took my hand and began leading me back down the hill. I pretty much guessed that we would now have to find some kind of shelter for the night. If it wasn't for my sister taking the lead then I would have been happy to just sit and wait up on that hill forever and day or at least until someone came and found me or I eventually just faded away into dust and bones and the wind carried me away to a better place.

Chapter 12

We walked in darkness for a good few hours that night, letting the stars and the bright light of the half-moon lead our way through the pitch-black countryside. We were so lucky that it was such a beautiful, clear sky. Some of the books our father had given us to study over the years had been about astronomy and celestial navigation—how the old sail boats and ships from the past few centuries, way before digital maps and satellites, had navigated their way through the seemingly never-ending oceans at night, using only the stars and constellations as their guidance.

We wanted to keep south—well, southeast to be precise—so we always knew to look out for the plough first and foremost if we ever found ourselves lost. Find the Big Dipper, or the Big Frying Pan as we liked to call it. Draw an imaginary line from the pan's outside edge, not its handle, and you should come very close to the last star in the Little Dipper, or the Little Frying Pan as we also liked to say. The last star in the Little Pan's handle is the North Star. So, as long as it was a clear night, we could take our bearings from that.

When we came to a row of three cottages, with only two of them with their lights switched on, we decided to take a closer look. We crouched down low and approached the first lighted window in the row. An old couple sat watching tv in the first cottage. The second cottage had their curtains fully drawn so we couldn't get a decent look at the people inside.

The third cottage had its curtains sprawled wide open. There were no lights coming from anywhere inside that we could see, and the cosy wee cottage seemed to be fully furnished too. We discussed breaking a window and climbing inside for the night. My sister convinced me that there was no one home or coming home anytime soon. Even the fire place looked as though it hadn't been used for quite some time, something she'd cleverly spotted with her keen eye.

I, on the other hand, still needed much more convincing than that, so I egged my sister on to take a closer look around the back of the secluded property, just for peace of mind more than anything else. I really didn't want to take any unnecessary risks. Again, we didn't find anything that gave us any suspicious, second thoughts to deter us from breaking into the old cottage and holing ourselves up for the night.

My sister was going to use her own t-shirt rolled around a half brick we found lying around in the backyard to break a small section of the back-kitchen window. But I'd noticed that the small, frosted bathroom window around the side of the cottage seemed to be slightly ajar, by no more than a centimetre or two at most. It was enough for the trained eye in the dark, like ours, to see that it wasn't fully locked. And with just enough room to dig our fingernails into the tiny gap and then slide our fingers even further within, using both our strength combined, we were able to pry the stiff window wide open enough to wriggle both our petite and skinny little body frames inside.

We found a living room, a double bedroom, a bathroom, and an empty kitchen lying in wait. The fridge was disappointingly bare when we eventually stumbled across it hidden in a darkened cupboard at the far end of the kitchen. We dared not to turn any of the lights on though, to see our way, for fear of being discovered by someone passing in the night or by one of the neighbours still awake watching their late night tv shows.

We were so damn hungry, but we bided our time and patiently waited until the lights went out in both the other cottages before doing anything about our hunger pangs.

After an hour, we opted to try the old folks' cottage, the first cottage in the row. Their front door was securely locked, but when we tried the handle of the door around the back we found it unlocked just like most isolated homes out in the wilderness and countryside, which we'd quickly come to discover for ourselves living out in the secluded highlands.

Inside the old folks' cottage, we made sure to be as quiet as we possibly could. The back door led straight into their kitchen area anyway, so that was one less thing to stress about. Again, without turning on any lights, we found and opened their fridge freezer and took out about half the contents inside, from cheese, tubs of soup, cold meat, and ginger ale. When we raided their kitchen cupboards, we also found some bread, cake, and biscuits.

We took our new stash back to our own cottage and very eagerly had ourselves a nice, little, dark, and quiet midnight feast before eventually falling asleep together on the large double bed in the main back bedroom.

I must've slept for a good few hours when I woke up suddenly in the middle of the night to such a fright. It was still so dark all around, although the break of dawn couldn't have been too far away. I felt the soft lips of someone or something kissing my cheeks, then my forehead, then my lips, then back to my cheeks again, in one continuous motion, over and over again.

At first It felt good and warm and nice all over to be awoken like that, and in my hazy dreams it was the face of James Brewster that I saw, my old schoolboy friend, who was hovering over me, gently kissing me awake from deep dark slumber. In the dream I had been running through a thick, dark forest before suddenly falling down a deep dark hole in amongst the trees. James had then appeared above me before climbing down the hole to try pull me back out again. But when I'd found myself paralysed and couldn't stand or even move my body in the slightest, to stop me from freaking the hell out and calling for my mum to come and help me, James, without any words, had just smiled one of his warm, dimpled smiles before covering me in warm delicious kisses all over my face.

When I jolted awake and swiftly realised that the feeling of being kissed all over my face was not, in fact, a dream but a chilling reality in the eerie darkness of the night, a disturbing shiver rippled through my spine, from my neck all the way down to my tailbone, and my entire body seized up in micro seconds.

I eventually opened my eyes only to be confronted by the most horrific and terrifying ghostly face, with thick, horrid, black lips and thick, round, black eyes. Huge evil eyes, to be exact. I wanted to scream to the high heavens, but I dared not even move a muscle for fear of what this horrible, chilling demon-creature might do to me.

Then I noticed the long, raven hair on this ghostly image, not too dissimilar from my own jet-black locks. When I finally blinked a few times, just to see if I could make the ghostly apparition disappear, my eyes slowly adjusted to the darkness and I was able to see that the face of death hovering over me and smiling warmly was in fact none other than my mischievous sister.

She chuckled hard, then backed up onto her knees, jerking away from my lying and frozen-with-fear frame. She clapped her hands hard too, then covered her mouth once more just to stop herself from screaming with laughter.

My eyes were still wide with shock and horror. What a transformation she'd gone through. And what the hell had she done to her face? She chuckled some more at my startled expression. She said she'd never seen me look so terrified before in her entire life, even compared to the night before when our father had wanted us to kill that poor woman down the back of the dark alleyway. What a difference a day makes, I thought. So easy to laugh and joke about that disturbing event now.

When my heartbeat began to relax down to its normal state, I sat up and composed myself a wee bit better. I asked what the hell she'd been up to? She told me that she couldn't sleep and that she'd eventually become fed up with nothing to do. In her bored state of mind, she had then nosily meandered next door, to the middle cottage this time, opened their unlocked back door, and wandered inside for a rummage around. The woman who lived there had all kinds of various make up and face paints stashed away in her cupboards, so she'd taken some of the white and black makeup paint, come back to our cottage, and painted her entire face ghost white, with black borders around her eyes and lips, like some kind of hideous and freaky zombie-ghost child.

I shook my head in disapproval, yet even that couldn't stop me from finally forcing a smile. What a crazy character she could be at times. When she insisted on painting my face the same way as hers, her new survival adventure face, she'd called it, I found her insistence too hard to resist. Her enthusiasm for doing spontaneous, crazy acts, was very infectious.

Once our faces were both painted the same, my sister then said that we should leave soon, at least before the sun came up. But before we left we should go back into the old couple's cottage and gather some more supplies for the day ahead. I agreed and we both wandered back inside the old folks' cottage again. We put all the supplies that we thought we might need into an old carrier bag, filling it to the brim this time. Then my sister unleashed the most mischievous look in my direction. She told me to put the bag down in the middle of the kitchen for the time being and follow her. We'd come back for it soon enough.

I didn't want to. I felt the knots forming inside my stomach at just the mere suggestion of following her even deeper into the old cottage. I just wanted to leave with our bag full of supplies and get a good few hours head start before the old couple realised they'd been robbed of most of their food supply. But my sister swiftly pulled me from the kitchen and into the old couple's living room then towards the closed hallway, before finally emerging in front of their bedroom door.

When she put her hand on the door handle, I immediately froze up. I didn't wish to go inside in the slightest. No way. Not a chance. I didn't want to do anything to these poor old people whose only crime was to gullably leave their back door unlocked. The knots in my stomach doubled, then tripled, making me feel extremely anxious and bloated with fear. My sister shushed me though and gently creaked open the bedroom door before quietly leading me inside.

The room was so dark at first, but I could clearly hear someone's loud snoring almost immediately upon entering. As we approached the bed, I just assumed it was the old man making those deafening and horrific snorts, but I was shockingly surprised to discover that it was in actual fact the old woman.

My sister was trying her hardest not to break out into a fit of giggles. She even tried to mimic the old lady by making her own pig-like snorts. I hit her a slight dig in the ribs for that. But it just made her giggles even worse, almost hysterical in fact. She even began crossing her legs and saying that she was gonna pee herself real soon with laughter. All the while the old couple didn't even stir an ounce at our racket.

As my sister moved ever closer towards the bed, I still had no idea what we were doing here or what the hell my sister's intentions might be towards the couple. I thought we might just stand over them for a while, watching them sleep, and make fun of them for a while or until my sister got bored and decided that enough was enough. But no, as soon as my sister had positioned herself right beside the old lady's upper body, she softly began shaking the poor old dear awake.

I felt absolutely mortified by my sister's actions. What the hell was my sister up to? Why was she trying to wake these poor old people up and get us caught in the process? My delayed reactions were far too slow to stop her though.

The old woman suddenly stirred in her sleep as my sister continued to shake her awake. The old woman gave out one last distorted snort before opening her eyes, fully wide and staring up at the crazy, twin ghost girls standing beside her bed.

A chilling silence filled the air. Then my sister unleashed a sinister grin and whispered the word 'boo'.

The old woman began screaming hysterically like nothing I'd ever heard or seen before. The old man jolted awake too with a startling fright and I swore, for one frightful second, that they were both gonna have a heart attack or a stroke and drop dead, right there on the bed where they both laid screaming their lungs out.

The old couple continued screaming before throwing themselves into each other's arms.

Credit to my sister though, she didn't get nervous or even think about giving the game away and running like the wind, straight out of the place, which was exactly what I desperately wanted to do. No, she kept her cool and maintained her ghostly act, even when the old woman started making the sign of the cross and raving that death had finally come to take her away.

My sister then lifted her arm, painfully slow, and pointed it, not at the old lady, but directly at the old man instead. Which made the old woman scream and howl even louder. My sister then took me by the hand and, almost in slow motion, led me out of the bedroom, leaving the door wide open behind us.

When we reached the kitchen, my sister burst out laughing. Then we ran. We grabbed our bag of goodies from the kitchen and ran like the clappers, jumping over the back-garden fence, over the surrounding fields and straight into the dark woods up ahead.

When we reached a small clearing deep within the forest, daylight was finally breaking through the patchy grey sky above us. We decided to sit down in the clearing for a while, just so we could catch our breaths and have a good munch from our goody bag. None of us said a single damn word. We just sat there and ate in total silence, listening occasionally to the sounds of the forest, like the awakening, singing birds and the light wind whistling through the trees. What a fright we would have looked to anyone who might've stumbled upon us at that moment.

A mile out from the forest and we came to another single-track road. It was tarred and littered with passing bays, so it appeared to be a well-used road. The sun was out, but we were surrounded by nothing but grey. Everywhere we looked, the sky was covered in a blanket of miserable dull. The only thing that could've made our morning anymore worse was rain but, strangely enough, for such a cloudy sky, the rain never came.

Nevertheless, we followed the road eastward where we knew the rising sun would be. We didn't have a particular plan of action in mind but to walk until we reached the sea on the east coast or a large town, then assess our options once we arrived there.

We needed to get back to the mainland, first and foremost. So that meant a need for a boat of some kind, or at least a sneak aboard one to make it back to the main land without drawing too much attention to ourselves. But with our faces still painted as they were, that feat was going to be easier said than done. At my sister's insistence though, she refused to allow either of us to wash the face paint off.

When the first car we'd seen, since our father's car the night before, passed us by, my sister didn't even glance up at it or try to wave it down, which I thought she might since she seemed to be the one who was much keener than I to make it back home quick smart, just so she could impress father more than anything.

But the car didn't even stop or slow down for that matter, even just to check or ask if the two little girls with the strange, painted faces walking by themselves in the middle of nowhere, on a downright cold and miserable morning, were both all right.

As soon as the car sped by, I made a darting glance to the rear of the vehicle only to see a happy and smiley looking wee boy and girl, much younger than my sister and I, glancing curiously back at us.

No less than ten minutes later, I heard another car fast approaching us from behind. This one was slowing down though. I could clearly hear it doing so. Then a small, two-doored vehicle pulled up alongside us. A handsome young man, perhaps in his mid-twenties or younger, was the only occupant inside. He wound down his driver's side window and smiled warmly out at us. He asked if we were okay walking along the road all by ourselves. At least my thoughts and prayers were answered and there still seemed to be some kind and caring souls left in the world who would go out of their way to check up on the safety and well-being of two little girls.

I'd already halted in my steps to acknowledge the young man just as soon as his car pulled over beside us, but only after he'd begun calling to us did my sister finally stop in her tracks and turn around to face him. She didn't say a word though. She just morbidly stared at him without even blinking, which kind of freaked me out, especially with her ghastly-painted face.

This chilling act didn't seem to faze the young man in the slightest though. Even when neither one of us replied to his questions at first. In fact, he didn't seem to mind our cautious silence one bit and just shrugged it humourlessly off before skipping on to ask his next question: where were we going?

He had a funny accent when he spoke. It was deep and friendly but not of this land. When he said the word 'where' he pronounced it more like 'vare' replacing his W's for V's.

My sister still didn't say a damn word, so finally I took it upon myself to step forward and speak with the young handsome man. I told him that we were at a friend's party the night before and were now heading back into town to our home.

"Is that vhy your vaces are all painted like ghouls' little ones?" he said with a cheery laugh. "Halloveen is still zo many months avay, no?"

I didn't know what to say to that, so I remained quiet like my sister. He asked why our parents hadn't picked us up from our party. I said that our parents didn't like to be bothered sometimes and that we do this walk home all the time, so it's no bother to us or them.

"I zee.' he replied, pondering hard. 'I think I like this liberal outlook on parenting in Scotland. It reminds me of my own upbringing. Oh vell. Zo, do you vant a lift into town, scary ghost children or do you just prefer to valk the rest of ze vay?" he continued in his upbeat jest ways. My sister then turned her attention towards me for a short moment before, without words, she nodded her head and motioned for me to get into the car with the strange speaking young man.

When the young man saw that we had accepted his offer of a ride, he immediately opened his driver's side door and stepped out before putting down the front seat and beckoning us to climb on into the back.

"I take it you are ze quiet one, huh?" he stated to my sister but she never said a single word back I reply. Instead she just gave him a long, hard look of daggers. "Very charming. And you must be ze talker I take it?" he said, returning his attention to me. I forced a smile and politely nodded before climbing in after my sister.

While he drove cheerfully along the lonely country roads of the Island he told us that he was a tourist from a country called Germany. Apparently, he was on some gap year from the University of Berlin exploring Europe. In the more remote regions like Scandinavia and Scotland, he'd decided to rent a car and drive around the countryside instead of busing or hiking it.

He then asked how old we were? I told him the truth, that we were both thirteen.

"Zo, not quite children anymore," he said, not really a question but more like a statement. He then asked us why our faces were painted that way? I told him it was to do with the party. He asked if it was fancy-dress party and I said yes. He then asked us what our names were. I didn't want to say, mainly because my dad had drilled it into us from an early age to never ever reveal our names to anyone that we did not already know. So, I kept very quiet on that matter.

"You do have names, don't you?" he insisted.

I just shook my head and said no, which seemed to amuse the young man somewhat and even made him chuckle.

"Fair enough," he continued. "I vill just call you Little Ghost Girl One and Little Ghost Girl Two. My name is Herman, by the way."

For a few minutes there was a long lull in the conversation. The young German man, Herman, whistled out a tune every now and again, but he left the radio off. For a few blissful minutes it seemed like he had forgotten all about us sitting there in the back of his car, hopefully bored from the lack of response to his questions.

But then suddenly and completely out of the blue, he looked at me in the rear-view mirror and asked if any of us knew what sex was?

I was a little taken aback by this comment at first, but then strangely eased a little by the casual and harmless way he'd just come out and said it, like he was asking us if we knew the name of that mountain lying in the distance up yonder.

To keep the casualness flowing I said I'd heard some things about it at school. He asked, but not eagerly, what things I'd heard? I said, just things and pictures from friends and teachers. He asked what kind of pictures. I said just animals, like dogs and rabbits, and funny wee stuff like that. Like when the dogs' mate and their little hind legs and backsides go into a rampant, epileptic fit of overdrive. He seemed to like that answer and chuckled at it too.

Next, he asked if either one of us had ever seen people mate like animals before. I said no. I'd never even thought about it before that very moment. I didn't even think it were possible or that it was something that people did, if I were brutally honest. What I did know was that the young man was starting to make me feel a little uncomfortable now with all the mating talk. But perhaps German people were just bold and forward like that when it came to discussing things that now, looking back, seemed very inappropriate and adult like to talk about with underage teenage girls. But I didn't know for sure at the time.

My sister, on the other hand, didn't seem that bothered by the strange tidal turn of conversation in the slightest. I didn't even think she was listening to a single word of it, to be honest. She seemed so focussed and transfixed on watching the passing scenery on her side of the car while seemingly lost in her own wee world of thoughts.

Herman stopped talking again for a short while, which I welcomed a great deal. He seemed to be really concentrating on the road up ahead, which was fine by me. Even when he took his eyes off the steering wheel to look and stare hard at some dirt track turn-offs that passed us by, I still didn't mind. I really enjoyed the peace and quiet. As much as people said that my sister was the silent type while I was the talker of the two, I still hated answering questions.

All of a sudden, Herman pulled into an old, dirt track lane that seemed to satisfy his fidgeting. It was hidden from the main road by some thick towering bushes. I was beginning to feel a little worried as I didn't think we'd be stopping again until we'd reached the next town, the one that he said he was heading to himself. My sister was still staring obliviously out of her window, even when Herman switched off the engine and turned fully around to face us in this new, secluded spot. She still didn't move or react one bit.

"Do you mind at all if I take off my trousers now?" Herman said with a big warm smile, like it was the most casual and natural thing to do in the whole wide world. Neither my sister nor I said a word, although my sister did finally scrape her eyes away from the window to give me the most surprised then mischievous of looks. The way she was seated and turned towards me though was completely out of Herman's view.

Herman then proceeded to pull down both his trousers and his underpants to reveal a very bushy jungle of pubic hair along with an almost completely hidden little penis in amongst it. He then calmly sat back against his driver's side door, while looking at me head on, before gently starting to stroke and play with his little penis, which strangely began to stiffen and grow larger as it gradually emerged from the horrific amount of bushy pubic hair it was hidden within.

Neither my sister nor I had ever seen a male penis before, not on a man or a boy. We'd seen them in books and then for real on some dogs and cats a couple of times, but never on any people, especially our own father, who always seemed to keep himself well and truly covered at all times while around us. Even while out on our camping adventures, he always made a great effort to wash on his own or go out deep into the woods to do his private business.

To be honest, I didn't expect a male penis to be so bloody hairy. It was like a dark, thick hedge with a strange little sausage-like thing poking out from the middle. I thought it looked absolutely disgusting and unnatural and completely uncivilised.

The more Herman touched himself though, the bigger and stiffer his wee little, strange, sausage like thing seemed to become. It looked so horrible that it actually made me want to throw up again.

My sister had to cover her mouth though in order to stop herself from laughing hysterically out loud. When she started to shake her head with disbelief, I suggested to her with my eyes that we should at least leave the car and be on our way and leave Herman to his strange and inappropriate carnal act. But she gently shook her head again while unleashing the most wicked and devious of grins.

"Do not be worried... or alarmed girls," Herman said in between gasps of pleasure as if sensing my nervousness and unrest. "I vill not touch you. It is not my style. Just knowing you are zare is more zan enough for me. I svear it... And I svear to drop you off, varever you vish to go... just as soon as I... ejaculate."

I had no idea what this ejaculate thing was that Herman seemed to be referring too, but I had no desire to stick around to find out. My sister saw the panic in me and calmly put her hand upon mine. She then gently stroked my cheek with her other hand and with a mischievous grin she whispered into my ear that everything was going to be fine.

My sister then did something most unexpected. For the first time in the young man's presence, she finally spoke. She asked him if she could climb into the front seat with him and take a closer look at what he was actually doing there. Herman looked a little taken aback by her genuine gesture. I was absolutely mortified that she'd suggested such a disgusting thing. But surprisingly, he agreed.

Without fear or hesitation, my sister then leapt into the front passenger seat and proceeded to take a closer, eager look at Herman as he continued to rub and stroke his wee bushy, frozen sausage but at a much faster pace.

He looked so serious and in such deep concentration that it almost made me laugh too if I wasn't feeling so downright anxious and disturbed. My sister couldn't help herself though and suddenly laughed and giggled at some of the more intense jerking and shuddering motions Herman was making.

"Please. Do no laugh," Herman cried, sounding a little frustrated and annoyed. "You are not supposed to laugh. I must concentrate here, very much… please."

But his intense, serious reaction, of course, made my sister laugh even harder. She asked what the hell he was doing and why he was making such funny animal noises and bizarre facial expressions.

"Fuck you, little Scottish bitch!" Herman cried in anger as his face, then his whole body, began contorting and turning shades of purple and red that I never knew were possible on a person. "I am… trying to… ejaculate here."

My sister shook her head again, but more in pity than in any kind of disgust or disbelief. She giggled again, then asked Herman if he was sure he should be doing such a strange and unruly act in front of two little girls. Herman just ignored her and started moaning out even louder, but he didn't seem to be in any kind of pain that I could make out.

My sister then asked what would happen if she tried something. Again, Herman ignored her words and started rubbing and beating his little sausage even harder. I thought my sister was going to ask something even more disgusting, like could she touch it too, but what happened next turned out to be something more shocking that I could ever imagine.

My sister casually pulled out her hunting knife, still tucked firmly into the belt of her jeans, and while Herman's eyes were closed tightly shut, looking and acting like he was in some kind of wild ecstasy, my sister sliced her knife right through the root of his stiff penis, cutting it completely off from the rest of his body like it were just a piece of hard butter.

The blood sprayed everywhere. I'd never seen so much blood spraying out from one single wound before in my entire life, even from the poor woman the other night. This must be an all-time record.

For the first few seconds, Herman didn't even realise what the hell had happened to him. Even when his sausage disappeared down the side of the seat and blood sprayed up and all over him, he still had his eyes shut while his hand continued to make that frantic up and down jerking motion with nothing but blood and thin air between his fingers.

For the second time in forty-eight hours I threw up, and all over the back seat of the car. My sister just cried out with a playful disgust.

Herman, coming to his senses, gradually began to realise what the hell had just happened as the realisation slowly began to sink in. He started howling in shock at first, like a badly injured dog left for dead on the side of the road. Then he began roaring and screaming out to the high heavens. When he ran out of breath, he glanced in horror at my sister who, by that point, was covering her mouth again, not in shock or horror or disgust like me, but desperately trying to hold in her cruel, belly laughter at the man's insane reaction and discomfort.

Then he just fainted, I think. Or perhaps died with shock, right there and then. Either way, we didn't hang around much longer to find out. Within seconds we were both clambering out of the car via the front passenger seat, my sister laughing her sick and twisted little head off while I puked out again, this time while on the move and running through the long grass and thick bushes. Running and moving as fast and as far away as we possibly could from Herman the German and his blood-soaked car.

Chapter 13

This time we stayed well clear of the roads and made our way through the never-ending array of fields, hills, valleys, and forests. And just as the sun had gradually made its way down its cloudy horizon bed, did we finally emerge over one last hill to be confronted by both the cold, dark grey sea and a small, sparkly fishing town that we pretty much guessed was Stornoway.

From the top of the hill we could clearly see the ferry port and the fishing harbour way down below, so we waited until nightfall before making our way towards it. I suppose our plan was to find an opportunity to sneak our way back aboard one of the big ferries that were about to return to the mainland, or even to just try and sneak into the back of one of the cars or many lorries that were queuing up to board.

We stuck close together, moving through the shadows of the old town as we made our way closer towards the main port. We hid behind stationary cars, bins, and lorries, well out of sight of any nosy people walking by, until it was safe to move on once again. When there were too many people around, we side-trekked down some dark wee alleyways just off the main street, trailing along their dark, old, stone walls and filthy pillars until we emerged back into the light again like little vampires still afraid of the fading sunlight.

It was so much easier to move freely around after sundown and not be discovered and questioned by strangers, even though we were still painfully slow in approaching our target destination. But then, in one careless move, we ended up giving two old men a fair good fright along the way.

They were standing around, smoking and sipping a pint of beer outside one of the murky, hidden harbour pub-caverns that looked somewhat like an abandoned building at first glance. We weren't paying the slightest bit of attention to what was in front of us when we walked straight into oldies from down another dark alleyway on the other side of the building. We were both too busy glancing back the way we'd came after stumbling across a drunken tramp urinating against one of the back-alley walls. When he turned to leer at us, he didn't say a word, just half smiled and nodded before turning his attention back to the dribbling act of nature's call. We were still a wee bit worried that he might try and follow us when we bumped, smack-bang, into the two, old drinkers.

When they saw our ghastly ghost faces, they jumped and shrieked, worse than any scared little kids I knew, before dropping their cigarettes and half-full pint glasses to the stone-cobbled floor, smashing them to smithereens instantly. We took flight immediately and were long gone from their sights by the time they'd gathered their wits to shout curses and dog's abuse in our direction.

When we reached the rear side of the dock, we snuck behind a large block of seemingly unused trailers. It wasn't too far away from where a long and narrow row of trucks and cars were still queuing to board one of the larger docked ferries in the port.

After a few minutes of waiting around and working out our next move, we finally saw an opportunity that had been sitting right in front of our very eyes. We'd heard some sheep bleating out, every now and again, from inside the huge trailer we'd been hiding up against. We didn't think too much about their cries at first, and it wasn't until my sister turned to gaze at me with another of her sly winks and mischievous smiles—like she had everything that was happening to us under her full control - that we swiftly realised our plan of action.

My sister pulled me by the arm and led me swiftly towards the gated end of the trailer. Lucky for us, the gate wasn't sealed by any padlocks, keys, or chains. It was just bolted shut. It took a fair bit of force to loosen the three bolts, which were all stiff and rusty as hell, but we managed to wiggle them free before pushing the huge gate all the way open.

Inside, the sheep ran away from us as fast as their little legs could carry them and huddled up against the far side of the trailer pen. So, my sister grabbed me by the hand again and made me run with her, at full speed, right into the heart of the foul-stinking trailer, to growl and howl at the sheep like we were a pair of mangy, starving wolves, scaring them into fleeing outside for their lives. It worked like a charm and, within seconds, most of the sheep had all charged out of the open trailer and into the main dockyard.

My sister and I cautiously followed them out, but instead of following the sheep into the open port space, we ran and hid behind the next trailer and watched with humour in our eyes and baited breaths as the whole entire dockyard came to a chaotic standstill. Every single worker on the harbour front, along with most of the security guards, were now sprinting and clambering around after the escaped sheep and trying their best to contain them. It was going to be a long night for most of the workers there for sure. Even better, the crazy event started a chain reaction of car drivers and truck drivers all exiting their vehicles, some of them to help, while the others just took pictures and had a good chuckle to themselves and each other as the sheep continued to run amok.

With every man, woman, and child's attention in that ferry port firmly focused upon the rampaging sheep, my sister and I had no problem whatsoever in sneaking aboard the nearby ferry. Which, in all fairness, could have been sailing to anywhere in the world that night, for all we knew. All we could do was slip aboard and ride our luck with the journey. It was turning into quite the exciting adventure though, no matter where we ended up.

Keeping low and crouching cautiously in-between cars, vans and lorries, we watched as another huge but jolly-looking truck driver exited his vehicle and made his way to the back of the ferry so he, too, could have a peek at what all the fuss was about.

It was a great big truck this large, jolly-looking man was driving. The largest of all the trucks we could see on board the ferry by a country mile. My sister wanted to have a quick wee glimpse inside the front cabin, just to see if it would be a decent place for us to hide. It looked spacious enough from the outside, but she wanted to see if there might be any good hiding spots within before we searched elsewhere.

It was hard work, to say the least, but we managed to climb up the steep-laddered, steel steps of the truck and into the huge front cab compartment. At first glance it looked so cosy and warm inside and, to me, it felt absolutely thrilling to be so high up and off the ground, so imagine how it felt to actually sit up front and drive the damn thing.

There was a massive William Wallace curtain behind the main front seats too, acting like a blanket barrier between the front and the back of the cabin. When my sister pulled the curtain to one side, well, you could have blown me away like a feather in the high winds. It was like a tiny wee studio flat back there. There was a chair, a table, a single bed that doubled as a couch, a small stove, kitchen worktop, a kettle, and a fridge—a well-stuffed one at that, with all kinds of various processed foods that we were never allowed to snack upon back home in a million years. It all looked so amazing and not like the inside of a lorry at all. I could imagine myself living there for the rest of life, it felt so snug and cosy.

My sister then pointed down underneath the makeshift couch and bed. There seemed to be plenty of room for the two of us to fit underneath there. We both smiled and nodded. We'd found our own little, personal, warm, and cosy hiding place for the duration of our stay on board the ferry.

An hour later and the ferry finally left the harbour. My sister and I were still hiding underneath the couch bed, while the big, jolly-looking truck driver was now back in the front seats of his truck. He was watching some comedy tv show or movie on a portable laptop and laughing so hard at almost every single word being uttered by the actors, that it made me want to giggle and laugh aloud, too, even though I had no idea what on earth he was watching.

My sister wasn't laughing though. She desperately needed to use the bathroom, so she was pretty much cursing the large, jolly truck driver for every noise and breath he made, a constant reminder to her that he was still inside the truck and was going nowhere for quite some time.

After another hour, the driver finally fell asleep. His laptop was still on but he was snoring like a constipated walrus. It was impossible for my sister to move past the huge driver though in order to make her way outside and find a bathroom somewhere. So, while I kept an eye on him through the half-drawn curtains, my sister grabbed a hold of one of his small pots from underneath the sink and worktop. She then placed the pot on the floor and proceeded to squat over it to do her business. When she'd finished, she picked up the pot and poured the contents down the wee sink and drain, before placing the pot back where she'd found it—regretfully unwashed since the noise of the running water might wake the sleeping driver.

The driver hadn't moved or twitched in the slightest though, just the sound of his loud monotonous snoring continued to fill our ears. While I kept a further eye on him, my sister went for the fridge. Quiet as a mouse, she took out some ham and cheese and passed some to me too before eating a little for herself. She placed the cheese and ham back inside the fridge compartment and took out some chocolate yogurts next. We couldn't find a spoon without making a decent amount of noise, so we just used our fingers instead to scoop the chocolate goodness out of the plastic carton before shoving it into our mouths like we were babies. We kept the empty yogurt pots stashed well underneath the bed.

We must have fallen asleep a little after that because the next thing I knew I was rudely awakened by two, huge stomping feet moving around the cabin in front of me. It was the driver. He was fully awake and making himself a coffee and a sandwich by the look of things. I watched him open then close the fridge door a few times, taking things out and putting them back in. He didn't seem to notice at all that some of his food stash was missing – a curse of having too much food in your kitchen anyhow.

When he'd finished his food preparation, he laid down upon the couch bed right above us. Thank Christ it was a pretty sturdy bed. I expected him to at least squash us to the floor just a little, since he was such a big guy, and maybe even wake my sister in the process, but the mattress hardly even budged an inch, which was a much-welcomed relief let me say.

For a few minutes more, I listened to the sound of the man munching on his sandwich then slurping away on his coffee. When he'd finished, he placed the cup and plate – a plate with still a wee bit of sandwich left upon it, down on the carpeted floor right in front of me. When he started snoring, I cautiously reached out and ate the rest of that sandwich.

A short while after, I fell into a deep and blissful sleep myself.

When I awoke again, the truck was moving. I could feel the vibrations of the wheels on solid ground right beneath us. It was daylight outside too. The truck driver's William Wallace curtains were about three quarters drawn so I could just about see the tip of some rugged mountain terrain out through the main front window, along with a lot of light grey sky.

I got the biggest fright of my young life though when I soon realised that my sister wasn't lying beside me anymore or anywhere that I could see for that matter. In fact, she didn't seem to be inside the truck compartment at all. *Where the hell was she?*

I couldn't see the driver. His entire body was blocked off by the curtain. With no lights on, the back cabin where I was still hiding underneath the couch/bed was fairly dark, with the only light coming in from the driver's window on the other side of the curtains. So, I decided to take a huge risk and gently crawl out from underneath the bed. I didn't need to be too quiet as the roar from the truck's engine and road below blocked out most of the sounds that I made, clumsy or on purpose.

Once I sat upright in the middle of the cabin, I did a kind of slow, 360-degree pan around the cabin. *Where the hell was that sister of mine?* All kinds of crazy scenarios started swirling through my anxious mind. Had the driver somehow caught her and dragged her out of the cabin, handing her over to the authorities somewhere? Where she hadn't said a single word about me and now here I lay, all alone in the back of some strange giant man's truck that could be on the road to any part of the British Isles.

Or had the driver found my sister and brutally butchered her, before dumping her body right off the next bridge? Or since we were clearly not on the ferry anymore, perhaps my sister had snuck out of the truck at some point to fetch something or to have a wee look around, only she couldn't manage to make her way back inside the truck again.

Jesus Christ, Dad was gonna be well pissed if we got separated or lost. My mind was in all kinds of paranoid twists and turns.

Suddenly, all my worries and prayers were swiftly answered and all at once too when I glanced over at the upside of the driver's couch/bed. The same one we were both supposed to be hiding under. I felt a little shocked but not totally surprised to find my sister crashed out on top of it.

I quickly crawled over towards her and whispered in her ear for her to wake the hell up immediately. When that failed to rouse her from her deep slumber I took it upon myself to shake her into consciousness, gently at first then more violently. Jesus Christ, she could sleep for Scotland this girl!

Her ghostly-white face paint was still mostly intact, if not a little smudged on her cheeks, so when she finally opened her eyes wide, she gave me such a startling fright, making me jump back and almost falling onto the floor unbalanced.

When I regained my composure, I asked her if she was all right and what the hell she was doing on the driver's bed all exposed and out in the open. She said that she'd woken up in the early hours, disturbed from her sleep by the movement of the truck driving away from the ferry. And once the driver had turned off the cabin light and began driving along the main roads, she'd decided that it was pretty much a safe bet to move up to the free, comfy bed above and get a few more hours kip.

I told her that she was absolutely crazy. *What if he'd caught her?* She just shrugged her shoulders and nodded down to the handle of her hunting knife that she happened to be lying upon and hidden in plain sight. I had to bite my tongue at her arrogance and stupidity. What else could I do?

Again, we were both hungry. We didn't want to risk opening the fridge another time since the light might catch the driver's eye. There were crazy amounts of crisps stored in the bottom cupboard but, again, we thought the noise of the scrunchy bags and crunchy crisps might catch the driver's attention. So, we munched on what was left of his loaf of bread instead. Once we'd filled our bellies, it was suddenly my turn to adhere to nature's call. So, I did exactly what my sister had done earlier that night and peed inside the small pot.

We then sat on the bed/couch together and watched the view of the scenic road out in front of us through the gap in the curtains. We tried our best to catch any wee glimpses of road signs so that we might find our bearings, but it was too awkward to get close enough to the curtains to focus on the outside without making ourselves known to the giant up front.

After almost two solid hours of driving, he finally pulled the truck over into a secluded petrol garage and service station. My sister nudged me and told me to get ready to leave just as soon as the driver exited the truck and disappeared from our sight. The driver stopped the truck right beside one of the first big pumps strictly to be used for lorries only.

He switched off the engine. I waited behind the curtains with baited breath. My sister just stood beside me, unemotional and unconcerned as she picked little tiny pieces of dirt and blood from underneath her fingernails. The driver was just about to exit the truck when he suddenly stopped. After the most excruciating and intense pauses, the large, jolly truck driver, called out into the back cabin, which sent the biggest of shivers right down the back of my spine.

"I'm gonna grab some breakfast guys. A good and proper, well-cooked Scottish breakfast. Would you guys be interested in joining me or can I bring you something back instead? Will you guys even be here when I return?" the driver said, finishing with a wry chuckle.

Both me and my sister froze. Who the hell was he talking to? Was he talking to us? Surely not. Was there someone else inside the truck? Someone who we'd missed or who had climbed in while we'd both been asleep?

I was about to say something when my sister shushed me. I then watched in horror as she gently gripped her large hunting knife and pulled it out, just a little from her belt.

"I know you're hiding back there, girls," the driver continued with another cheerful chuckle. He had a funny accent too that I couldn't quite place. "I saw you both sneak in, way back on the ferry, before we even left Stornoway."

I glanced at my sister with wide, cautious eyes. Eyes like that of a deer trapped in full beaming headlights. She let out a deep sigh and gently took her finger away from my lips. I let out a deep breath too and, taking a hold of my sister's hand, we both revealed ourselves from behind the curtain.

Chapter 14

The Jolly truck driver's name was Chris. His body was huge and bulky, somewhere in between fat and muscle. He was well over six and a half feet tall, with naturally tanned skin, a big, bald, shiny head when he took of his baseball cap, and a larger-than-life beaming smile. He reminded me of that American wrestler one of my old friends from school had shown me a picture of once. The Rock, I think was his name. But Chris was a badly out-of-shape version of him. If Chris had a nickname, then perhaps it might have been something like The Abnormal Potato.

Like I guessed, he wasn't Scottish and had a strange accent, with a much lower tone of voice than you'd expect from someone of his sheer size and presence. His English was perfect, just a wee bit funny to listen too. Like some bulky, freak of nature and hyperactive cartoon character with a high-pitched voice. He said he was from Romania originally, but had lived in Scotland for the past twenty odd years, first to work on building sites, then eventually as a truck driver once he'd saved up enough money to attain his HGV license.

He told us all this as we sat opposite him inside one of the dozen or so booths in the quiet, little, service station café where his truck was parked out front. He told us we could order anything we liked on the menu. So, we did and ordered two, small Scottish breakfasts and two strawberry milkshakes. I knew it was twice in as many days that we'd ordered the milkshakes, but we honestly didn't know when we'd ever get the chance to taste them again once we'd made it back home.

Chris ordered a large strawberry milkshake for himself too, along with two extra-large Scottish breakfasts. I'd never seen anyone eat so much before in one sitting in my entire life. He was a freak of nature for sure but in a good, cool, and decent way.

My sister, as usual, sat in complete and utter silence, glancing out through the window, occupying herself with her own thoughts until her breakfast came. Then she sipped excruciatingly slowly on her milkshake before finally eating her breakfast even more painfully sluggish and slow as Chris and I chatted amongst ourselves.

Well, Chris mostly did the talking and I listened.

I liked the way Chris didn't push us for answers for the most obvious of questions right from the get go, like, where were our parents and why the hell were two little girls sneaking onto a boat and hiding in his truck in the middle of the night. You know, like the usual adult, twenty question, interrogation. But the more I got to know him, the more I realised that he was just a big kind-hearted kid at his heart, so much more of a kid than my sister or I had ever been or could ever hope to be. And I really liked that about him.

I asked him why his head was so big, round, and bald for someone who seemed to be so young—early forties or, perhaps, late thirties. He chuckled at that. In fact he chuckled after answering almost every single question I asked him. He said that he inherited that trait of his body from his father and grandfather before him, who had both gone bald in their twenties, and that the large women of his family always had a habit of squeezing out big, giant-like babies. So, he had his mother's genes to thank for his huge, bulky frame. He said that his older brother was even larger than him, which I found extremely hard to believe until he took out an old picture from his wallet and showed me. I nearly spat out my milkshake when I saw the two of them standing side by side.

He told us some funny stories, about growing up in the Romanian Mountains, that kind of reminded me of my sister and I growing up here in the Scottish mountains. There was one story: while both he and his brother were out camping in the Carpathian Mountains—of their own free will and not forced to do so by their crazy lunatic father might I add—when they were attacked in the middle of the night by a huge brown bear. They were both in their late teens at the time, so had almost fully grown into their monstrous sized bodies, although the bear that attacked them was almost twice Chris's size once it was fully up on its two hind legs.

But with the two of them working together, they were able to wrestle and kill the bear with their own bare hands, which I thought was mightily impressive. I even imagined my sister and I achieving the same feat if we ever came across any bears here in Scotland. Although, we'd probably use sticks and knives and any kind of good, sharp weapons that we could get our fingers on rather than our own bare hands. In fact, the more I thought about it, the more I was convinced that my sister could take care of the bear all on her own with her outdoor wits and skills, even without my assistance.

Chris told us about his driving job which took him all over the UK, and that driving around Scotland was by far his favourite thing to do in the whole wide world. He was in love with our stunning, scenic Highlands, our never-ending array of lochs, endless rocky cliffs, and white, sandy-beach coastlines. He said he had the most perfect job he could ever hope to wish for: doing something he loved, driving around such a beautiful country, and getting paid bloody damn well for it too. He said he couldn't be happier and I believed him.

I asked him where he lived in Scotland. He said down in the Central Belt, just outside a little old town called Falkirk. He said he had a Scottish wife, now, along with a son and a daughter a few years younger than my sister and I. Sometimes he took his kids with him on his long-haul driving jobs up North but only during the school holidays and if they really wanted to come along, which he said they usually always did.

He said he never forced them to do anything that they didn't feel like doing. He enjoyed giving his children and wife the freedom and opportunity to make their own choices and decisions in life. Something that I couldn't relate to, not even a little. But I never told Chris that.

Oddly, he didn't ask us about our painted faces either for quite some time. Well, not until we'd finished our food. The waiter who'd brought our meals over gave us a funny wee look, which my sister took full advantage of by giving the waiter a sinister grin and a foul hard stare of her own in return. She must've looked like a right wee psychopath.

If only he knew the half of it.

When Chris did mention our painted faces, it was more in a positive statement about our appearances than a baited question.

"I like your painted faces," he said with another chuckle. "You remind me of two, little, wild warriors. Like those ancient and fearsome Scottish Picts, you read about in Scottish history books, you know. The ones who used to paint their faces all white and blue. Do you think I'd suit my big, round face painted like yours?" he said with another jolly chortle.

I told him, yeah, absolutely, he probably would. Then he said that he would sometimes let his own daughter draw and paint his face too, whenever she was feeling creative and wanted to experiment her creativity upon him. He said he even let her paint his face with a big Scottish flag one time. She even made him promise not to wash it off until he came back from his next delivery trip. Which to the odd looks from his clients and other drivers on the road, he was true to his word. He chuckled again at that and so did I. I didn't think he was lying in the slightest. I could really believe that he would do such a thing for his daughter—a show of affection from a father was something I could only dream about.

It made my heart swell with such pride yet burst with so much sorrow at the exact same time. Proud that there were some fathers out there like Chris, who could love their daughters unconditionally and, in a way that they were supposed to be loved and cherished. Sorrow, because it was sadly too late for me in this life to experience anything like that from my own father.

My sister just gave me an evil glare when she caught me smiling and giggling too much at Chris's story. However, I ignored her for the time being and asked Chris where he was heading off to next. He said he was taking a big delivery up to John O' Groats, the furthest, most northern point in the whole of the Scottish mainland, then picking up another delivery on the way back down in Inverness before taking that delivery further down to Edinburgh.

My heart skipped a beat at the very mention of the word Edinburgh. I told Chris that I'd always wanted to see that city— that I'd heard so many good things about the gorgeous, gothic Old Town and seen so many great pictures too. He said it was just as beautiful in person as it was in those pictures. Hell, even more so once you'd greedily seen it all with your own eyes. He sounded like my dad for a moment, while trying to explain the beauty of the place, but I didn't mind. Beauty could be gazed upon in the same light by black hearts as well as good ones, it would seem.

As Chris paid the bill for breakfast, he asked if he could drop us off anywhere in particular. I asked him about our whereabouts, which hadn't occurred to me to ask about until that very moment. He said we were in a wee place called Lairg. Kind of halfway between Inverness and John O' Groats in the far north eastern part of Scotland.

I told him where we stayed. Well, the nearest town to us that he might've heard of… Arisaig, which was still a good bit away from our coastal home. Chris knew it at once and said that he could drop us off there, no problem, but it would have to be on his run back down from John O' groats and Inverness. If we weren't in a big rush then he could have us there by the late afternoon of tomorrow. I said I'd have to discuss it with my sister first since she had the final say in pretty much everything that we did, which he completely understood.

So, my sister and I swiftly nipped into the women's toilets to discuss this new side trek in our hectic adventure. There was nobody else inside the large toilets as far as we could tell, but we locked ourselves into one of the vacant cubicles anyway. I told my sister that I'd like for us to travel the rest of the way with Chris. I liked him and trusted him and really wanted to get to know him more. I felt safe around him and knew in my bones that he wouldn't try anything dirty or insane or anything inappropriate or out of the ordinary, unlike the last weirdo, Herman the bloody German, who'd been the last person to pick us up.

For a second, I wondered if he was all right, Herman. Had he made it to some kind of hospital to get the desperate aid and medical attention he severely needed for the brutal wound my sister had inflicted upon him? How would he ever explain such a thing to the authorities? Would the doctors be able to sow his little penis back on and make it all better and work normally again?

Secretly, I hoped not. I hated to think such a bad thing about someone, but it was the thought that he might try something like that again on another group of unsuspecting, innocent victims. But then again, perhaps he'd just simply bled to death inside that rental car of his. His body all hard, cold, contorted and soulless by now, still lying there undiscovered in the secluded layby. I guess I'd never know, and that actually seemed okay too.

My mind switched back to Chris and the debating conversation I was having about him with my stubborn sister. She said that she didn't care for him at all. That he reminded her of some big, dumb, childlike orc, held back a few years from school. Although, she did feel in her bones and admit, too, that he was utterly harmless and, right then, seemed to be the best, easiest, and quickest bet of getting back home in such a short space of time. And if that was going to be tomorrow afternoon then it would still be in record time. I think a week, our father had said, was his best going on foot. And that's what my sister really cared about more than anything: to make our own good father proud, to impress the man who treated his daughters like they were nothing more than animals to be trained and discarded at his own will.

My sister finally gave in and agreed to let us travel with Chris. I was thrilled to bits and could have kissed her cheeks numerous times, but I knew how much she hated anyone touching her, even me, her own sister, unless she was the one who initiated the contact first.

She said that she didn't mind sitting in the back while I kept Chris company up front. If he tried anything, anything shady at all, then she would be the first one to slash his throat, gut out his flabby belly, and feed his insides to the nearest farm animals. I completely took her at her word for that too.

Chris's big, round, smiling face was already waiting for us back at the truck. He'd bought a huge goody bag of supplies too, from crisps and sweets to juices and fizzy drinks for us to snack upon. I stayed in the big seats upfront while my sister skulked off into the back.

Chris eventually asked for my name, but I said I couldn't tell him just yet. I'd known him for only a few hours and he was still practically a stranger to me, which he agreed with, too, and completely understood. I also told him that once I was sure in the pit of my stomach that I could trust him, without any shadow of a doubt, then I would tell him my name, no problem.

I heard my sister snort and fake-gag at that in the darkness of the cabin behind me. But I didn't care. When I finally glanced back at her, she was already lying down upon the cabin bed again with her back turned fully towards me.

As we continued to drive along the quiet highland roads, I asked Chris why he hadn't called us out when he'd first seen us sneaking into his truck or at least called the authorities on the ferry to come and take us away.

"It wasn't my business," he swiftly replied, more serious in his tone than I'd heard him thus far. "You both obviously knew what you were doing. You hadn't been forced to get inside my truck. I thought maybe at first you were trying to run away from something or someone, but you didn't look scared and you definitely didn't seem to be under any kind of duress. In fact, you both seemed to be in total and complete control of your actions. Although, do you wish me to take you to a police station or a hospital or something?"

That was when my sister spoke out in Chris's presence for the very first time. In fact, she yelled her answer that we were to be taken to no hospitals and no police stations. We were just on our way home, that was all, and that our parents knew exactly where we were and what we were up to.

"There you have it then," Chris responded with another of his big, beaming smiles, as wide as the river that was now stalking alongside us. "Who am I to interfere with that, huh? You may look like kids at first glance, but inside you most bloody well are not."

A long pause lingered in the air. It wasn't uncomfortable in the slightest, just nice and normal and welcoming. Then Chris spoke again, wearing another of his huge cheesy grins.

"You guys didn't have anything to do with those rampaging sheep back at the harbour last night, did you?"

I desperately tried not to smile. I desperately tried to keep a strict, straight face for as long as I possibly could. But the way Chris was still grinning mischievously at me, I just couldn't help but smile right back at him.

"I knew it!" he roared, followed by a belly laugh that was so loud I thought both his stomach and his face were going to explode at the exact same time. "You girls are so kickass crazy."

Chris continued to drive further North while talking about himself and his life and all of his wonderful adventures in Scotland and back home in Romania. How his brother was a retired professional boxer back in his homeland. How they had both saved up and bought their own few acres of land in the countryside there, along the same mountain heartland where they had grown up as children. And how, when his kids were all grown up and old enough to leave home, he would retire from his life in Scotland and return to Romania with his wife to start building a new home on that land.

I was just happy to sit there and listen and take in all of his crazy, wonderful tales and dreams, if I was honest, which always seemed to end on a happy, positive note. My sister was right; a big, happy, fun-loving dumb kid was the best way to describe the jolly giant of a man.

Chapter 15

An hour before sunset, Chris pulled over onto the banks of a stunning and picturesque loch. He said we could take half an hour there to stretch our legs, eat some snacks, and maybe have a paddle in the water too before taking on the last hour of the journey to John O' Groats.

Once he'd picked up his new load, he'd buy us a nice dinner at a fast food restaurant before grabbing a few hours kip in the truck; we could sleep longer if we liked, as Chris would then drive through the remainder of the night back down to Inverness and then to our home.

It was a calm, clear, and humid evening beside the quiet and peaceful loch, even though the sun was low in the sky and on its final descent into the horizon's abyss, leaving nothing but a beautiful array of pink, red, and fiery orange trailing in its wake.

My grumpy sister was the last of us to leave the shelter of the truck behind, but the first of us to rush down the pebbled, rocky shores of the loch, barging past Chris and I like we weren't even there, on her way into the calm and cold waters without any fear or hesitation. Then without words or even a glance back at us, she began kicking off her shoes and stripping off her clothes—jeans, trainers, socks, hoody, t-shirt—everything, leaving nothing but a trail of abandoned garments in her wake. Wearing only her knickers to cover her modesty, she ran harder and faster into the clear, smooth waters of the loch before diving underneath the cool, calm waves.

Where most people would hesitate wading into new, uncharted waters, my sister had no fear of them in the slightest. Day or night, she loved the water and she loved to swim. When we were swimming in lochs together or down by the sea coast beside our home, that was when I saw my sister at her happiest and most free. Even if her unphased and unreactive body language was telling everyone else around her a completely different story. Her actions spoke far louder than any words or any blank facial expressions that she constantly gave off. And right then she was very comfortable in her surroundings.

Chris and I hung back not far from his truck, just off the edge of the quiet and secluded slip road on the banks of the loch shore, and watched with completely different emotions as my sister swam further and further out into the water.

Chris was laughing giddily again but feeling mightily impressed that such a young girl could just go and do something like that, something that most adult men and women could not without a care in the world or a second thought for her environment and surroundings.

I, on the other hand, was just feeling a little apprehensive. My sister was as unpredictable as she was unfriendly and uncaring to people that she did not know. I had no clue if she would swim around the loch for an hour or so, come back in a few minutes, or just swim over to the other side of the water and disappear into the thick isolated forest there, never to be seen nor heard from for a good few days at least, well, not until she turned up at my father's farmhouse again.

"As we say back in Romania," Chris started, interrupting my anxious train of thoughts. "I like the big brass balls on your sister, man. If you don't mind me saying." He shook his head, still in disbelief of her actions. "The water must be so bloody damn cold in there!" He screeched. "It would take at least a thirty-degree mini heat wave to make me even consider taking off all my clothes and go skinny dipping into a Scottish lake."

I told Chris that she does it all the time. That *we* do it all the time. Even amidst winter. However, I began to seriously doubt that I still would if it weren't for my sister right beside me, egging me on. I think I'd be much happier just lying on the shore with a good book or walking around the beach, exploring the rugged and off beaten paths and terrains rather than wading in for a swim. Swimming adventurously and freely without a care in the world was my sister's pastime and idea of fun, I quickly realised, not mine. I felt no obligation to follow her into those waters, in the slightest, unless we were desperate and had no other place else to go. Like we were trying to escape and hide from something or someone terrible or we were trying to catch some fish to eat for a meal. Even during a quick bathe or wash when we we're camping out, the pain of the freezing cold water against my naked skin far outweighed the pleasure of having that clean, fresh look on my body and hair after the act.

Plus, by this time tomorrow I would be enjoying my own warm and soothing bath and shower back in my own home again. So, delaying a bathing session by another day or so was never going to be a big deal for me.

"She's a bloody mysterious one, your sister, no? She doesn't like to say much but at the same time, she has such a demanding aura and presence about her, no?"

I told Chris that she had always been like that for as long as I could remember. She inherited her bold confidence and feisty arrogance, if you'd like to call it that, by taking after my father a hundred percent. And as far as being quiet, well, she could talk when she wanted to or if she had something that was well worth saying. But at her core, she only really talked to me or my father. A larger percentage to me though.

Even at school the teachers could barely get a word edgeways out of her, even on a good day. But because of her intimidating body language and facial expressions and her callous cold hard stares, oh, if looks could kill then the whole entire school would be gathering dust by now. And because of who my father was, the teachers never made a big fuss about her strange and awkward behaviour or pushed her to speak or read openly in front of the class. They'd just let her get on with it and do her own thing. Let her keep on being silent and broody, but at the same time keeping her almost out of the way, seated in the far back corner of the classroom so she could watch, stare, and listen as much as she liked without intimidating any of the other kids or teachers around her.

When dad eventually pulled us out of school, I think that every teacher in the place was a little relieved deep down inside. Thankful, too, that they wouldn't have to deal with or tolerate her cold, hard, and brooding demeanour any longer inside their classrooms, and grateful that she was somebody else's problem now.

And the more time she spent in the company of just me and my father, I think the worse and more unsocial she became. Strangers, or people she did not know very well, who entered our lives, even just for a few fleeting moments, she always treated with the utmost suspicion. She always looked upon new people, trying to pry their way into our lives, as a threat that could eventually lead to taking one of us, either me or my father, away from her. Or, potentially, both of us. Which is why she hated with a vengeance any new friends I made at school or out and about around the country, and so acted up accordingly. Which is probably why she was being so aloof towards Chris and I, retreating even further into her cold hard shell.

But what could I do? She was my sister and I loved her with every ounce of blood and fibre in my being. I just had to let her get on with it. She was a force of nature. The biggest and meanest force of nature I'd ever witnessed in my entire life.

From my words, trying to explain my sister's strange and erratic ways and actions, what Chris took most of all from it was my sister's close relationship with my father.

"Your father... He must be very special to your sister then, if she puts him on the same such pedestal as you—her own twin sister, no?"

With a slight burst of unfamiliar anger, I replied to Chris that my greatest fear was that she might actually place our father on a much higher pedestal than the one in which I was already seated upon. But he just shook his head and said that he couldn't believe it. That he wouldn't believe it. That a brother' or sisters' bond was always going to be far stronger than the bond between a father and his child. But I knew that he could only speak from his own experience, from his own perspective. He had no idea what it was like to be me, to grow up the way I did, no more than I had the faintest clue about what it was like to be him.

I wanted to tell him about my mother too. About my thoughts, opinions, and theories of what became of her. About that woman in the cellar who I believed to be her but was forbidden to say out loud, even by my own sister. Those dead frozen babies that my dad kept as some kind of trophy or memento. But I just couldn't find the words. There was no way I could confess such an horrific thing to anyone. I mean, where the hell was I to start with that?

Then for some reason that I couldn't explain, I confessed to Chris instead that if it wasn't for my sister I would have run away from my father's grasp a long, long time ago. I didn't mean to say such a thing, but my emotions were getting the better of me, especially since I hadn't talked like this to anyone before in my entire life. I wasn't as good as my sister you see at keeping my feelings and emotions bottled up, deep down inside.

But as soon as I'd said it, I completely regretted it. It was such a naïve and stupid thing to say in front of someone who I'd only just met. I'd let my guard down. Surely now, the prying questions were about to flow from Chris's mouth due to the obligation he might've felt about our situation, which in his mind must have been growing ever more curious and bizarre the more I opened my mouth to talk.

He'd have a growing suspicion and urge now to try and protect us, protect *me*, or at least take us and hand us over to the proper authorities, if he sensed even just a wee bit that something was amiss and foul in the air regarding my relationship with my father.

Instead though, he surprised me somewhat, he just stood there in silence and continued to watch my sister's bobbing head, moving further and further away from our view, out into the loch.

The more he just stood there in silence, though, not moving an inch, keeping completely still, only breathing his deep, hard breaths, the more I noticed the sun making his huge, bear-like shadow, gently creep over me like some kind of invisible, protective shield.

"What would you have me do?" Chris finally said, breaking the unbearable silence between us. "Would you like to talk about this… this father of yours… or would you wish for me to just forget that you ever mentioned him and how you have always wished to just … runaway?"

His spoken words made everything so damn real. To hear him repeat them back to me, sent sharp, terrifying shivers straight down my spine. So, I had told him a partial confession. I hadn't just imagined telling him something.

And with that sudden realisation I began to feel the emotional brick walls that I'd built up over the years begin to topple down and crumble away, just like that. With no warning whatsoever, nothing. It just happened. It crept up on me like the dawn of a new day. Like I'd closed my eyes in the darkness of night for just a few moments and—bam! When I reopened them again, the light was already there. That was how quickly my dams had burst and collapsed within and the tears soon flooded right out of my body and soul.

Then I did close my eyes, tightly at first, to try and make the tears stop. But it was impossible. Absolutely impossible. I felt them trickle down my face without end. Yet I dared not even move a muscle in order to wipe them away and give Chris the impression that something terrible was wrong. Yes, I would do everything in my stubborn power to not draw that kind of attention to myself.

Like Chris, I stood on the edge of the slip road, watching my sister disappear across the lake, yet positioned just slightly ahead of him. I'm sure he saw my entire body tense and stiffen up within the rays of the setting sun but, thankfully, he couldn't see the unstoppable tears rolling down my cheeks. If he ever did, then I knew in a heartbeat that everything would change. Which is why I was trying my hardest to keep looking directly ahead, to keep watching my sister, to remain completely still and focused and calm in my posture, to not even make a peep nor sound for appearances sake.

Then I felt Chris's hand upon my shoulder. It was a gentle giant's touch that threw me completely and melted my body at the exact same time, while sending more tingling, soothing shivers, shooting down my spine.

"Are you okay?" he asked.

In that instant, I'd never wanted to turn around and hug someone so much before in my entire life. Just to turn into Chris's arms now, bury my face, head, and body into his ape-like, warm belly and chest and strong, strong arms to unleash an avalanche of tears and a lifetime of pent-up frustrations, emotions, and sobs. So many things that I'd never even done before: to hug, to cry, to reveal all of my vulnerabilities and insecurities to another human being, to let go of everything and let him see me.

But before Chris could even finish that sentence or start another, my prickly defence mechanism kicked in and I ran. I ran as fast and as hard as I possibly could, straight for the hard-pebbled beach shores of the loch.

Like my sister before me, I swiftly whipped off all of my clothes, leaving only my underwear on until I was wading, ankle deep—then knee deep, then thigh deep, then waist deep—straight into the bizarrely comforting but freezing cold waters.

Tears were still flowing down my cheeks like a never-ending waterfall bursting from behind my blue eyes. I dared not look around or back at Chris. Not yet. Not until I could get my head and face fully underneath the water to quickly wash away all of those painful, pesky tears. Those tears that gave everything away—my whole life story in one devastating glance—if he looked at me now.

I dunked my head underneath the crystal-clear, ice-cold water. I stayed under, like that, for such a long time. For as long as I possibly could until my inhaled breath desperately began to rip its way through my chest and lungs with its restrained claws.

Finally, when I could take the pain no more, I burst up and out of the water and breathed again. Breathed that good, hard, beautiful, clear air through my lips, into my mouth, down my throat, and into my frozen lungs like I'd been given a second chance at life. But when I placed my hands to my face, unbelievably, those same warm, salty tears that I so desperately wanted to be rid of were still there. They were still coming, thick and fast.

This time I didn't fight them.

Instead, I took it as a sign. A sweet, long, hard, relieving sign, that I should swim back to Chris. That I should go back and confess to him everything. Everything about my brutal, miserable life that I wanted to tell him so much after he'd first rested his supportive hand upon my shoulder.

I took a deep breath and finally turned around. I turned back to face Chris who was still standing on the slip road, back over on the other side of the shore, looking strangely bemused and, dare I say, hurt by my fleeing actions.

Yes. That's exactly what I was going to do. I was to tell him everything about my father, my mother, my sister, and I. Our miserable, shitty life and existence together. About a mother I never knew, whose ghastly, open grave was beneath my feet all this time, throughout every step of my upbringing. An ever-growing tumour-like suspicion that turned into fact, about my father's involvement in her imprisonment and eventual death.

And then I'd let fate take care of the rest. And if that meant my sister and I could go home to live with Chris for a wee while, to be welcomed into his loving family with warm, open arms or even be passed around from one foster home to another for the rest of our teenage days, never knowing who was going to be our next parents from one year to the next, then so be it. Anything was better than the alternative. Going back there to *him*.

Anything.

And then it happened. Like some kind of mad, freakish hallucination or a dream-turned-nightmare—a terrifying apparition—I saw my father and he was coming towards us. Coming towards Chris to be precise.

Was I seeing things? Had I stayed far too long underneath the cold, calm waves that my oxygen-starved brain was now playing dirty, nasty tricks on my vision and mind?

And then I saw my father lunge at Chris from behind. He was holding a big, sharp, silver blade in the hand of his firm right arm. A blade that briefly glistened in the setting sunlight, but not for long. No, not for very long at all as he swiftly plunged that knife deep into the spine of Chris's back. Not once or twice did he make this vicious action, but a dozen. A hundred. No, a thousand times, it seemed. Over and over again. One vicious stab after the next.

I saw Chris—my big, happy, humble, and gentle giant—topple down onto his knees, with his hands and arms stretched out, his gaping mouth wide, but for all the water still in my ears, I couldn't hear his painful, roaring screams. Perhaps there were none and he was just gasping for the last ounce of life left in him.

Then the redness came. It slowly seeped over then through him. Over and through his bright-yellow t-shirt like some cancerous, creeping branch of evil, seeping over his entire body from every possible angle.

I didn't know how, but I shook myself awake from my paralysed state. I started screaming, screaming and howling like I'd never done before. I never knew that my lungs were capable of such a deafening and horrifying shrieks and sounds. Then I swam and ran, both at the exact same time, desperately trying to make the quickest exit movement from the loch back to the shore, back to my Chris. Back to my dying Chris.

When I looked briefly at my father, he appeared nothing more than a raging, wild demon unleashed from the pits of a bloodied hell only he knew existed as he continued to stab and slash, slash and stab at Chris's back, over and over.

I neared the beach with a sprint towards Chris who had fallen like an enormous thick oak tree, flat on his face and onto the mud and grass at the bottom of the slip road where it met with the pebbled shore.

No, no, no. I screamed over and over again. I ran past my clothes, even my trainers, barely giving them a thought. My bare feet were cutting themselves to shreds at the soles on the hard rocks and jagged pebbles.

"Fucking paedo, bastard, scumbag!" I heard my dad rage. "Trying tae take advantage of ma two wee girls, ye fucking paedo fuckwit bastard ye."

I continued to scream. No, no, *no.*

"Well, yul think fuckin twice noo, aey, ye fuckin dirty cunt bag."

I ignored my father and dropped straight down onto my knees, right in front of Chris's big, bald, warm head, which seemed like the only part of him that wasn't covered in his own blood. I tried to take his head in my hands but it was just too big and heavy for me to lift more than an inch from the ground. I begged him to get up. I begged him to turn around and look at me. I begged him to say that he was all right. That everything was going to be okay. That he would be with his loving family soon. That this was all just some crazy, terrifying, mad nightmare.

He gurgled and hissed. He was trying to breathe but his breath was just so faint and weak. The life was draining out of him at a million miles an hour. My tears started spilling onto the back of his head and down his ears. His breathing became almost nothing, non-existent. I didn't know what to do or say. My thoughts were a rabid mess of insanity. I thought of his beloved brother back in Romania, his wife, his children down in Falkirk that he would never get to see, hear, or play with again. His daughter who would never be able to paint his big, round, chubby, happy, beautiful face again. The land he had purchased back in Romania for his retirement yet would never get to make it his own.

I thought about how this was all my fault. I should have known better than to accept his generosity. I should have been more like my sister, cold and hard from the get go, and ran from him just as soon as he'd made himself known to us. *Thanks for the ride, but we've got to be on our way!* This is what happens when I let people in.

I didn't know what to do. So, I leaned my face and lips close to Chris's ears. I told him that he was a good man. That he didn't deserve this. That he didn't deserve to go out like this. I told him through my sobs, snot and tears how I wished that in another life he could have been my father. That I could have been his daughter. I didn't care if my own father, still standing over us, heard me or not. I even half expected my own throat to be slashed next for such blasphemy.

Then I whispered Chris my name. I told him my meaningless, insignificant, miserable, shitty wee name. But I think he was already gone by then. What light that was left in him had already long since faded from his eyes.

My father was still ranting and raving like the lunatic he was, pacing back and forth behind me. I wasn't listening to him in the slightest though. Then I heard more splashing down by the loch shore. When I glanced up and looked over with my tear-filled eyes I could just about see the blurry image of my sister emerging from the water. For a long time, she just stood on the water's edge, quietly observing the whole scene crazy unfold.

The speed in which she'd swam all the way back here showed me that she was both startled and concerned for my wellbeing after hearing my screams and cries. But my father's presence had turned her into an unemotional rock once more as she continued to stand and stare on the edge of the shore, both doing and saying nothing. If she did have any feeling for what had just happened here, then she'd never make those feelings known in front of my father. Which I completely understood and fully forgave her for, instantly. What the hell was she ever going to do against him?

My dad soon raged in her direction though as soon as he was fully aware of her presence.

"Whit the fuck are ye just standing there gawking fur, eh? Put yur fuckin claethes back oan and help me clean up this fuckin mess."

My sister swiftly did what my father asked and hurriedly put all of her clothes back on. Just as soon as she was dressed she went and gathered up all of my clothes too. That's when I felt the big, hard, excruciatingly painful kick from my father's right boot, slamming into my ribs with such awful pain and brutal force that it sent me tumbling further down onto the pebbled beach below. The sharp, violent blow, shocked and winded me severely.

"Whit the fuck are ye waiting for in aw, ye wee fuckin shite? Get fuckin dressed tae, ye wee cunt!"

I tried my best to keep my rage, tears, grief, and sorrowful cries inside. Swiftly, my sister approached and handed me my clothes. She lightly patted my head and hair, careful not to let her gesture catch the unwanted attention of my father's eye, before running back up the slip road slope towards his departing presence.

Using my t-shirt, I wiped my tears away as best I could and dressed myself in no particular urgency. When I was ready, I slowly made my way past Chris's lifeless body and towards the slip road, giving his sad, unmoving frame one last longing glance of sorrow.

From the bottom of the slip road I could see my father and sister both up and rummaging inside Chris's truck, clearing anything out that might belong to us. He then poured a tin of gasoline that he retrieved from the back of his car, around the inside and outside of Chris's truck. He then made all three of us drag Chris's stiff, heavy body, down to the water's edge before pushing him out into the loch to let the gentle, rocking waves carry him away.

As I walked back along the beach, deliberately trailing behind my father and sister, I turned every now and again to watch Chris's big, lifeless body drift further and further away. He looked like some small raft floating out to sea.

Dad then ordered my sister and I into his car, me in the back and my sister up front. We did exactly what he said, no questions asked. The last thing he did before driving us all away was throw a lighter into the truck's front compartment, letting the cabin ignite into a flaming fireball.

By the time we drove off the secluded slip road and back out onto the main road, a thick black smoke was already pouring up at a rip-roaring rate into the darkening and picturesque sunset sky behind us.

Chapter 16

Every now and then, on the long car journey back home, my sister made wee, sympathetic glances back to me, like she wanted me to know that she felt for me or that she shared my pain even though, deep inside, I knew she did not.

She always chose her moments to glance my way with great care though, like while dad was distracted by some other drivers on the road that were more inferior to the laws of the road than him, or singing along to one of his crappy and annoying music CDs, or glancing out at another stunning, scenic mountain range or a loch that had caught his eye on the horizon. The latter was something that I couldn't quite understand or fully comprehend. I mean, how on earth could a person full of such rage, hatred, evil, and destruction even begin to appreciate such beauty and wonder in the world?

By making me sit in the back of the car, all by myself, he'd made it very clear who he blamed for our little, off-the-beaten-track, adventure. As it turned out, dad confessed that he'd been following us all along yet had kept his distance from our unsuspecting sights. He also said to my sister, but loud enough for me to hear over his deafening music, that we'd also made him proud, especially by how we'd dealt with the young German tourist who'd picked us up. Yes, very proud indeed. Well, up until the moment when I'd decided to extend our adventure further north with the truck driver instead of giving thanks for the ride back over to the mainland and making our way south again. Back to our humble adobe in record time.

"I dinnae ken hoo many chances av given that sister of yours back there!" he blatantly ranted right in front of me. "Ah mean, why can she no just be like you, eh? Yur fuckin near perfect, ma lass. Fuckin near perfect, ye are. Like a fuckin soldier machine."

Still, my sister didn't acknowledge the praise or say anything in reply. She never did. She just kept looking straight ahead, out of the window and into the darkness, now that the sun's rays were fully extinguished.

"Ah mean..." he continued, ranting on and not really caring whether she was taking it all in or not. "If you were oot here on your ain wi-oot that wee cunt arse in the back there dragging at yur heels, yud be hame in nae time. You could have destroyed ma record. Nae bother. And ma da's record for that matter. And yur a fuckin lassie for fuck's sake!"

Dad chuckled and shook his head, like he couldn't quite believe that a wee girl of all people could be better at something than a man. An adult man at that.

"Gramps would be rolling aroond pishin in his fuckin grave right aboot noo if he kent his ain granddaughter was a better man than he—than fuckin I. A better man than fuckin I for that matter. And yur naw even a fully-grown woman yet. Fuck me yur gonnae be something special, lass. Something fuckin special indeed!"

My sister remained absolutely silent, just like she always did when dad heaped praise after praise upon her. But I'd never heard him lay it on this thick before. If I was honest, I'd say that deep down inside she was more embarrassed than proud. I would have been, that's for sure. In fact, I was. Was this how modern-day adults, really behaved? But what could I do, huh? What the hell could I do but listen?

When we finally made it back home a few hours before dawn, and just when the night was at its darkest, dad had another surprise in store for us. Instead of pulling up into the farm house, letting us inside and sending us both to our beds without a warm shower and without any supper, he oddly kept on driving. He drove past the farm house and down along the old, muddy back road. A road only ever used by passing tractors or four-by-fours with people brave enough to venture down them.

Dad continued to drive along the dark, coastal mud track, moving ever closer towards the thick forest a few miles south of our house. I wondered what the hell he had in store for us next. I knew my sister was wondering the same too. But where I was beginning to seriously tire of my father's challenges and spontaneous adventures, she seemed to be relishing in them as her eyes widened and her body became more alert.

None of us said anything regarding the burning question that needed to be asked though. My ribs were still aching and throbbing from dad's most recent hard boot imprints there and I had no intention of provoking another beating from him. If I had to best guess, then I'd say he was going to make us camp out in the woods again tonight or for another few days at least, as punishment for pissing him off.

He brought the car to a sudden halt just inside the treeline edge of the forest. He told us to get out. We did what we were told, again, without question. He popped the car boot up and we followed him around to the rear of the car. He pulled out a couple of spades and handed one each to me and my sister. Dad took out some thin rope, too, and slung it over his shoulder. He also grabbed some tape and a thin, metre-long, plastic pipe. A pipe I'd seen him use before whilst installing our new shower last year. He then slammed the boot door shut and told us to follow him, quick smart. And we did, right into the dark forest.

We walked about a good mile or so into the pitch-black woods. My sister and I walked side by side while dad continued to walk a few metres ahead of us. For a second, I thought about getting my sister's attention, either by taking her hand or gently tapping her on the shoulder and motioning her to turn and run away with me. I was sure that together we could both outrun and outsmart my father in these thick, dark woods. But I knew in my heart that my sister would never go through with it. She'd never leave father and come with me, even if she thought she could get away.

So, I swiftly put those thoughts to one side. How could we ever outrun and outsmart a man who always seemed two steps ahead of us at all times?

I shook my head and tried to distract my thoughts onto something else. For the first time since dad had brutally murdered Chris up at the loch, I realised that most of the white paint on my sister's face had disappeared, most likely washed away from her swimming expedition back in the water while Chris and I watched on from the shore. The paint on my face was probably washed away too, but I couldn't be sure.

Soon, dad came to a sudden standstill inside a small clearing surrounded by trees and bushes. I noticed the ground was very soft and muddy here, even a little slippery underneath my feet. Dad turned around. He threw his wad of rope and pipe down onto the dark floor, just in front of a bush, and told us both to start digging while he watched and supervised.

My sister and I glanced at each other for a short moment. We didn't understand what was going on, but my gut instinct told me that it wasn't good. Nothing that came out of my dad's head was ever good or had any long-term decent intentions. I realised that now. For the first time in my life, the urge to just turn and run from him, without my sister by my side, almost overwhelmed me into doing just that. The feeling was so great that I could feel a nervous bile rising from my stomach up into my chest. The urge to vomit finally got the better of me. I turned and puked into a nearby bush. My dad didn't say a word. He didn't need to. His expression painted a thousand words. He just glared at me with a look of pure and utter contempt before gently shaking his head with a great disgust.

My sister was the first of us to strike her spade into the soft dirt to dig. I think she did this to defuse the tension between me and my father more than anything else. I soon followed suit. As we dug, dad drew an outline, shaped like a rectangular box, around where we were digging. It was about five feet by two feet in diameter. The shape of a small coffin was my initial thought as soon as he'd finished making the mark. I knew then that this little late-night outing into the woods wasn't going to end well for someone—most likely me, but still, like a scared, brainless fool, I continued to dig.

When the hole was at least three-foot deep and five in length, dad made us stop.

He told us to put our spades down. Then he asked me to pick up the wad of thin rope by the nearby bush and bring it to him. I did as he asked. But as soon as I handed it over, he violently grabbed a hold of my arms with a vice-like, iron grip.

Startled and shocked by his actions, a delayed scream and yelp finally left my lips. As I struggled in his arms, he turned me around to face my sister who looked just as stunned and as shocked as me. He then asked her to take the rope from his shoulder and tie my ankles together, before binding my wrists right after.

I struggled out as frantically as I could with the dwindling strength of my lower body and legs. I could hardly move my arms and upper body as my dad's grip was so strong and fierce. So, I kicked out more and more with my legs and feet. Dad whispered in my ear that it would be easier for me if I just relaxed and let it happen, that I didn't need to struggle. That it was going to happen regardless, so I should be a good girl and just be still. Why make things harder than they already were?

But inside, I felt absolutely terrified. I couldn't let this happen. No way. I refused to believe that this was just another of his tests, another of his sick and twisted survival games. I felt that I was fighting for my life. Fighting for my sheer survival.

My sister, hiding her own discomfort well, took the rope from my dad's shoulder and brought it down towards my struggling lower limbs and kicking-like-crazy feet. She even hesitated for the slightest of beats, just enough to make my father's anger rise up and out of him, directly at her.

"Dae as yer fuckin telt!" he roared. "Tie her fuckin ankles, noo!"

With his new rage consuming him from the inside out, he intensified his grip around my arms and shoulders, squeezing his strong firm arms even tighter around me like some huge, wild, jungle snake. I could feel my chest and lungs being crushed into submission while my heart pounded in my mouth. The pain in my already-bruised or broken ribs increased to near-excruciating levels.

My sister saw the pain and discomfort I was in and swiftly began tying my ever-growing limp ankles and feet together. Once she had them securely tied, my dad forced both my wrists together and made my sister tie them too, tight and hard. As soon as they were bound, my dad released his firm hold of me and pushed me down onto the muddy ground. The horror and emotion of the situation suddenly became too much for me and I couldn't stop myself from crying and sobbing out again, just like I'd done only a few hours before, back up at the loch in front of my father, kneeling and mourning over Chris's lifeless body.

Dad picked up the roll of tape and leaned down towards me. My sister took a few steps back, still saying nothing. She was breathing hard. I could clearly see that she was upset. That this whole crazy charade was taking its toll on her too. But she didn't have a clue on how to act or how to handle the situation in front of my father. So, she did the easiest thing that came to her. Absolutely nothing.

I wasn't angry with her though. Far from it. If the situation was reversed I would have done exactly the same as her—absolutely nothing and remained utterly quiet, still and obedient and await further instruction from the man who'd instilled that fear and obedience into us.

As my father reached down to tape my mouth shut, I begged and pleaded with him, probably for the first time in my life, not to do it. I cried and sobbed for him to give me another chance to prove myself. To prove my worth. That I could be a better person in his eyes. *A better daughter.* That I could and would be more like my sister from that moment onwards. That I could make him proud, if only he would give me another chance. I was so desperate to live, to survive, I would have said anything, *done anything* in that terrifying moment.

I knew my words were all for nothing, but I said them all the same.

"Nay mare chances for you, ye wee shite," he said. "Yuv had years tae learn to be like your sister. Fuckin *years*, ye wee wining cunt. But aw yer dain noo is holding her back from showing her real potential. Every decision she makes she's aw-ways hesitating, seekin oot your fuckin approval first, or seein hoo it will affect you, mare than her. Yur the fuckin albatross aroond her fuckin neck, lass."

I continued to cry and beg for mercy, even though I knew in my heart it was the worst possible thing I could do and that all my sobs and pleas were only falling on deaf ears.

"Even noo, in this present fuckin moment, ye cannae even be like yur sister. Dae ye think she wid be sitting there noo, bawling her wee cunty girl eyes oot like a wee fuckin spoilt princess? Naw, she wouldnae! She'd be calm and collected and welcoming tae the next fuckin challenge!"

"Well, we'll see hoo ye dae wi this wee fuckin experience then. Noo, listen and *listen,* fuckin gid ma lass. Am gonnae drive your sister aw the way back up tae that fuckin island, back up tae they fuckin standing stanes. And she's gonna make her way aw the way back doon here as fast as she fuckin can again. Aw the while yul be stuck in that fuckin earth waiting on her. And if your sister is as quick and as smert at getting fae one side of the country tae the other, as I believe she is and wi-oot you holding her back like a fuckin lead balloon, then she'll be back tae dig ye up in nae time. Nae time at aw to stop ye fae freezing and suffocating tae yur whiny wee death!"

He then tore off a thick length of tape and let out another evil glare.

"Noo, ma wee fuckin angel, ye cannie get any mare fairer than that noo, canye?"

Before I even had the time to scream or protest or comprehend anything I'd just said, dad shoved the tape over my mouth, picked me up like a pillow, and threw me face up and onto my back into the dirt, into the coffin-shaped hole I'd just dug for myself.

He then picked up the metre-length piece of thin, plastic pipe and dug the bottom end forcefully through and into my taped mouth. He told me to grip it hard with my teeth and tongue and suck the air into it, and that if I didn't, well, I'd just suffocate in less than a minute.

With those last few words, he grabbed a spade and motioned for my sister to grab the other, then, together, the two of them filled the hole back in with the mud, dirt, and stones and proceeded to bury me alive in my shallow grave.

The plastic pipe inside my mouth had been pushed far too hard through the tape and into the back of my mouth though. It was beginning to make me choke hard, my eyes water, and my nose run. Thankfully, I was able to push it up and out of the back of my throat, just a wee touch, using the strength of my tongue. Now I could get a good suck of air from the hollow tube inside, which gradually began to calm my nerves.

Long deep breaths. I kept telling myself over and over again. Long deep breaths.

My eyes were still firmly shut and I dared not open them, even a little, for fear of all the dirt and mud seeping in through my eyelids. I could feel the soil continuing to cover me, layer after layer, from head to toe. It was gradually becoming heavier and heavier, weighing my body down more and more by the passing seconds.

I'd never felt so terrified and helpless before in my entire life. How the hell was I ever going to get out of this? If I didn't suffocate first or choke to death at some point then it was going to be another few days at least, maybe even a week, before my sister returned and I saw the light of day again. But only if she ever did return.

That thought wasn't even worth thinking about at that moment. I was going to be trapped down here, in the dirty, suffocating darkness until I slowly died of dehydration or suffocation, with only the slightest hope that my sister might get back in time to dig me out.

There was nothing else to it.

I had to accept my situation, and quick smart too, if I was going to survive this nightmare. I had to calm my breathing, calm my anxious thoughts and nerves and racing mind and just lie there, lie there still and wait. Wait for some kind of miracle in the eternal darkness. With nothing but the sound of my own breathing and my own thoughts for company.

Chapter 17

It was so dark in there, which wasn't even the worst part. I couldn't move an inch, *that* was the worst of it. Even just to scratch a wee itch that kept resurfacing on my left thigh, I would have given my right arm just to give it a good, hard scratch in that moment.

I thought about trying to move and wriggle. I really did. I thought about making one of those sudden, forceful, and continuous twist-and-turn movements, over and over, desperately trying to see if I could shake myself free from the heavy dirt and mud weighing down on me like a lead-ton weight. But the fear of losing my air pipe, having it slip away from the grasp of my mouth and being unable to recover the end of the tube and breathe again if things didn't go according to plan, while desperately trying to shake my way out of my shallow grave, well, it was more than terrifying. It had paralysed me once again into doing nothing but lie absolutely frozen-stiff, trying to ride out the storm in the best way I knew how: passively.

I just had to wait it out. That's all I could do. Then the more hours that passed, the more terrified I became of falling asleep and choking to death. It was funny how falling asleep hadn't even entered my mind when my father had first buried me down there. Now, it was all I could think about. *When* it would happen, not if. Would I ever awaken again if I did drift off, even for just a few moments?

At one point I let out a great, frustrated internal cry with my mouth firmly shut. It seemed to help. For a little while after, I began to think clearly again. Well, as clearly as any young, teenage girl, who'd been buried alive in the middle of a secluded forest, could hope to think.

I thought about Chris a lot. I blamed myself for his death, one hundred percent. I wished that I'd never gotten into his truck yesterday and that we'd just parted ways back at the petrol station café after he'd bought us our breakfast. I could almost imagine father watching us from the other side of the service station, then pulling his hair out after witnessing us accept Chris's offer of a lift, but driving further north first instead of heading south.

How could I have been so stupid? Of course, dad was watching us the entire time. Just like he'd done all those times before when he'd left us in the woods to fend for ourselves for days on end.

Why hadn't I realised that? Why hadn't I learned my previous life lessons concerning him? I swore to myself that if I ever made it out of this hell hole alive and saw daylight again, then one day I would do the decent thing and somehow track down Chris's family, his wife, his daughters and confess to them everything that had happened. Beg them for forgiveness. Tell them how he'd looked after me and my sister while we were under his care and protection. Tell them what a good, kind-hearted man he was. A heart that swelled with goodness and kindness and decency and joy. But I'm sure they already knew that. Without a shadow of doubt, they knew it.

I thought about my sister too. I wondered where she might be right about then. Was she still on her way back up to the Isle of Lewis with my father? Had she even started to make her journey back down again, yet? Had my father, perhaps, also tricked her into digging her own grave somewhere in the woods and had left her buried deep down in the suffocating darkness, too, until he felt the merciful urge to come and dig us both back up again once he'd decided that we'd had enough of his torturous games?

I had no idea about anything though. All I could do was speculate in my own mind where I was also a prisoner. All I had to go on was hope and fear, and fear was winning by a landslide victory so far. I tried not to think about dad, but it was almost nigh on impossible to prevent the image of his smug, twisted face and sinister grin from creeping back into my mind.

I hated him so much. I wanted him to die the most horrific and painful death. I wanted to inflict upon him even just a tiny bit of the pain and misery that he'd inflicted upon me and my sister over the years. I wanted him to suffer. I wanted him to hurt, mentally and physically. More than anything, I wanted him to hold me in his arms like a real, normal, loving father and tell me that he was so sorry, that everything was going to be all right. That it was okay to cry. That it was okay to be weak and vulnerable sometimes. That he knew he was very ill in the head before, so mentally ill, but he was better now, all better, and then he would cry too and beg for my forgiveness.

In my head I wanted desperately to forgive that man—that sad, weeping, apologetic monster. But deep down inside, I knew that I never really could. Even if that fantasy in my head ever did play out in reality. That's when the rage, anger, and hate overwhelmed me again. I began to imagine all the different ways in which I might gain my revenge on him. Most of those grisly ways involved a knife, a chainsaw, a pitch fork, a set of garden sheers, or all of the above.

But the long, slow, torturous death I loved best was the one that involved carving him open, bit by bit, piece by piece, peeling him slowly from foot to forehead like peeling the dry skin from a rotten apple so that he could feel and endure every second and every ounce of pain that I intended to inflict upon him.

As the minutes, hours, and maybe even days—who knew—dragged by, eventually, in the darkness, my mind began to wander into madness. Every single one of my senses abandoned me. I didn't know what time of day it was or even what day it was. How long had I been in the grave? I didn't even know if what had happened to me or what was happening to me still, was real anymore. I felt so delusional. So disorientated.

I imagined that I'd died ages ago and had been sent straight to hell and this was my punishment—to suffer an eternity in a weighted darkness with only my spiralling thoughts for companionship forever and ever. That was it.

Then the strangest thing happened. I thought I heard my name being called, but from far, far away. It sounded extremely faint at first. But then there it was again, I felt sure. Someone was frantically calling my name from some muffled and far off distant land above. Or was my mind just playing more tricks on me?

Then came the thudding and scraping and banging and raking. Then I felt the dirt and mud becoming lighter and lighter on top of my body. I thought I was dreaming. I was probably hallucinating. But I didn't care; the heart-warming relief felt so great. I thought I'd died and gone to heaven, yet it was more likely hell. I didn't care which though as long as the dirt got lighter, the voices got louder, and I could finally see the light of day again. I felt so desperate for something to change. For something real to come into my vision again and not just an image in my mind.

Suddenly there it was. A tiny bit of grey then white light. It was daytime out there, for sure, although I didn't care what time of day it was, just that it was there. Even though my eyes were still full of mud. Then came the hands, wiping more dirt away from my face. The tube piping pulled gently from my mouth, followed by the fingers on my cheeks pulling the tape—no—yanking it from my mouth and lips.

I breathed my first, long, deep, hard, and refreshing breath of good, old-fashioned clean air. Never had air tasted so good before. Never. I savoured every breath that followed. Over and over. Again, and again.

I felt the hands on my face once more. This time wiping more dirt and soil away from my cheeks and eyes. Then from my ears and hair. Like an angel singing, I heard my sister's voice calling my name and asking me if I was all right. If I was okay. Hearing her voice, knowing that it was her who had finally come for me. Come to save me. Hearing and knowing that she was there before opening my eyes to see her beautiful, angelic face was all I needed in order to be flooded with so much good emotions that I never thought I could possibly feel and all at the same time. I could have died right there, in that moment, for I'd never felt so happier to be alive before in my life.

I started to sob and cry. I couldn't help myself. The great relief of being free again was just too much, was just far too overwhelming. My sister hugged me. She told me that everything was going to be okay. And I believed her.

I never saw her pull out her knife but I felt it cutting the rope that tied my ankles together. She grabbed a hold of my bound wrists next and cut their ties too, slicing right through the thin ropes with hardly any effort. She pulled me up to my feet and hugged me so hard, so tight. I'd never felt so much love from my sister before, never. I didn't really believe it existed, or that such feelings could have radiated from her person.

When we finally pulled away from our embrace, my sister said that we should go quickly. She took my hand and tried to lead me away through some nearby trees. I stopped her though. With what little strength I had left in my body, I dug my heels into the ground. I told her that I wasn't going back to the house. That I wasn't going back to him. Never again. And if she wanted to take me there, instead of running away together to find a new place to live, a new home to grow up in, then she should bury me back in the ground again where she'd found me and just leave me there to die.

My sister smiled at that. She lightly cupped my cheek in her hand and said that she wouldn't have it any other way. I smiled too. More tears streamed down my face. A single tear fell from my sister's eye and rolled down her cheek before settling upon her lip like something warm and wanted.

She hugged me hard and promised me that she would never leave me alone again, never leave my side. That she would stay with me always. Always and forever. She would protect me from everything bad and evil in the world, including my father. That she would never let any harm come to me again. And if anyone or anything did try to harm me, then they'd have her to answer to, always.

Then everything started to fade. I felt the forest and trees, wind and earth, swiftly and violently yank my sister away from my grasp. It felt like the whole entire forest had just swallowed her up before sucking me right back down into that shallow grave once again.

Suddenly, everything turned to darkness. Then I felt a pair of large, firm hands grasping a hold of my wrists and painfully yanking me back out of the grave, once more, with an incredible ease.

To my despair, this felt more real than being dug out of the ground by my sister just moments ago. Someone big and strong was shaking me now, so violently hard. Shaking the dirt and muck right off of me. I felt the stinging pain of the tape being ripped from my lips. I could have opened my eyes, but I didn't want too. I instinctively knew what was in store for me out there without having to take a look.

I heard his muffled, rough, and ranting voice. Those same big, strong hands grabbed me hard by the hair, yanking my head and neck right back into an unnatural position before slapping me across the side of my face and ears. More dirt and soil fell from my earlobes.

"Are ye listening tae me girl, aye? Are ye fuckin listening?"

I heard his voice loud and clear. It was him. My father. Dad. He was the one who had dug me out of hell before projecting me into a new one.

"Ye didnae think ah was gonnae make it so easy for ye's noo, did ye? Eh? Eh? That yer sister was just gonnae make her way aw the way back doon here, dig ye up nice and easy, lemon squeezy, and that was gonnae be the end of it aw, aye? Back tae fuckin normality again, is that wit ye thought ye stupid wee cunt, aye?

I didn't answer. I didn't want to answer. I was in so much pain and shock and relief of being out in the open air again. For a moment, I thought that I might me dreaming again. That I might awake at any second back in that underground tomb. And if this was to be my new reality, out here with him, then I couldn't believe that I was actually thinking it, but I desperately did want to secretly wake up back inside that underground tomb again. I'd rather take my chances down there and wait for my sister to come find me than to progress further out there with anything that my sick father had in store.

I felt dizzy. I felt like I wanted to be sick again. Barely had the thought and feeling of nausea filled my mind when my father hoisted me up and over his shoulders in a fireman's lift. Still tied and bound at my ankles and wrists, he proceeded to carry me back through the woods. At that moment, I'd never wanted to be buried alive again so much before in my entire life.

Chapter 18

Dad bundled me hard into the back of his car and drove the short journey from the edge of the forest to our farm house home, just a few miles further up the coast. Lying with my face down on the backseat, I could hear a howling wind outside, bashing this way and that against every side of the vehicle. My restricted view out of the dark windows were blocked by an avalanche of rain that seemed to pour down heavier and heavier the closer we got to the farmhouse.

Dad pulled up close to the front door and exited the car, caring not a jot for the cruel, foul rain and wind whirling around him, pushing him this way and that, trying its hardest to keep him inside the vehicle. In my mind, I desperately imagined it was I who was controlling that horrific weather, using it to do my bidding and battle against my father, trying my bloody damnedest to blow him off his feet or up and away into the clouds then out into the freezing-cold sea. But he soon managed to open the back door and drag me out of the car, throwing me over his shoulder again before carrying me into the house.

I realised then that no vicious hurricane or howling wind was ever going to be a match against the determination of my psychotic father. Without pausing for thought or breath, he carried me all the way down to his secret cellar, way underneath the foundations of the house. The huge and heavy old oak bookcase that kept the doorway hidden had already been shoved to one side. He must have been planning this fate for me all along.

Once through the iron doorway at the bottom of the steep and narrow staircase, he plonked me down hard right in the middle of the first dark room we entered from the corridor. I held my breath as he pulled out a long, sharp knife and leaned with a sinister glee down towards me. He let me take a good, long look at its blade before, surprisingly, cutting the rope around both my wrists and ankles and not my throat, so that I was free to move, walk, or even crawl around the confounds of the large, dark cellar complex.

He must have felt fully confident that there was no other way out of the cellar for me, with or without the use of my hands and feet. Either that or he thought that I was far too scared of him and the consequences that he would reign down upon me if ever the opportunity to escape arose.

"Yul wait doon here like a good wee cunt until your sister returns. And if ah hear just one wee peep fae you before that happens, then al start slicing auf yer fuckin fingers, one by one. A finger for every noise ah hear coming fae doon here. And when ah run oot uv fingers, it'll be yur fuckin toes ah start oan next. Ye understand me, wee girl, aye?"

I wanted to scream at him. I wanted to yell and roar in his face just how much I hated him. How I already knew about his secret cellar. How me and my sister had discovered his dirty, little secret a long time ago. That I knew what he'd done to our mother down here - to our other dozen or so little brothers and sisters - I knew what he'd done, although I didn't understand why.

I wanted to roar at him, too, about how much I wished he was dead. How much I wished he would just drop down and die and be gone from this world and out of our lives for good. But I knew it would be the worst possible thing I could do in that moment if I wanted to see my sister again. He'd love that. He'd love the confrontation of it all and he'd love any excuse to beat the living, holy shit out of me right there in that cellar, for any anger and hate that I showed towards him.

So, I bit my tongue and said nothing. Not one wee word did I utter, only nodded that I understood him perfectly. I was to sit and be quiet and remain still while waiting down there in the cold, dark, damp cellar for my sister's return.

There was a long, silent, and uncomfortable pause before dad turned around to leave, locking the huge iron door behind him as he left. I wondered how long he'd let my mother live down here after my sister and I were born. I wondered at what stage of our infancy did she pass away. Had he killed her himself, with his own bare hands, on that mattress after he'd gotten what he wanted from her? Us I assumed—my twin sister and I. Well, that's what it looked like to me. But why us? And what had been wrong with the other babies. Why hadn't they been kept alive or given a chance to grow up like us.

Holy shit. The freezer?

It all rapidly flooded back to me like a gust of hurricane wind in my face. As my eyes gradually adjusted to the darkness, I tried to look around for it. The cellar was a huge complex of empty stone-and-brick-walled rooms underneath the house. Each room was eerier, creepier and darker than the last.

As I cautiously made my way from one room to the next, I eventually found the freezer again in the furthest most room from the main Iron door. Still exactly in its same spot from the last time we'd ventured down there.

The mattress was still in the same place too, but I didn't want to get too close again and check if the skeleton was still hiding there. In the darkness, I managed to pry open the lid of the freezer and glance inside, even though every ounce of blood and fibre in my being resisted for me to do so. But I had to check. I had to at least see if dad had kept his trophies, even after my sister and I had discovered them without his knowledge.

The freezer was empty.

For a second it made me question if those little bodies had ever been there in the first place. Had my sister and I just imagined it all? Surely not. *Definitely* not. Dad must have gotten rid of them since we were last here. Maybe they were buried out in the woods by now or thrown into the sea for fish food.

I shuddered at the thoughts running through my mind of what he'd done to those poor, defenceless creatures. I closed the freezer and backed out of the room. I'd find some other spot down here to dwell in. But not that place. Not that room.

I tried to sleep in the back corner of another cold, dark room but it was almost impossible. The hard-stone floor was just so cold and uncomfortable. It was even getting a little damp and wet with the torrential rain from outside somehow finding its way into the cellar and onto the floor through the cracks in the side foundations.

I was starving, too, and felt so thirsty. The food I could do little about, but when the rain worsened in the early hours of the next morning, I was able to drink some dribbles of water coming in from the cracks of the concrete walls and ceiling above.

Just before sunrise, I heard my father walking around the ground floor of the house above me, probably getting ready for work. He didn't even come down to see how I was doing or to bring me anything to eat, not that I even expected him to make such a kind gesture. He was holding me captive, after all, and I had no idea regarding his full intentions with me.

To tell the truth though I didn't want him to come back down to the cellar to see me. I didn't wish to see him again, full stop. In fact, I'd be happier if I'd never had to look him in his cold and heartless eyes ever again.

The following day passed by so painfully slow. It seemed to drag on for such a long time without incident nor sound. Nothing creaked or groaned from above. Nothing moved or made a sound in the darkness. The rain and the wind seemed to have died out altogether. Only my own breathing and subtle, weak movements seemed to disturb the silent darkness every now and then.

I felt glad that I was able to at least walk around freely down here and that I wasn't still stuck in that horrible, suffocating grave, unable to move or scream or cry out or even think straight. Even though I'd only exchanged one prison for another, I felt eternally grateful to be holed up in this much more spacious one now that I'd had the time to regain my wits and composure.

I kept wishing that my sister would hurry up though. That she would somehow find a way to rush back to the house and rescue me, whisking me away from this hell before my father returned to vent his wrath and punish us further in some other torturous way.

I knew my sister though. I knew that she would find a way back to me, by hook or crook, by manipulation or by force. But she wouldn't come straight to the house. No. I feared that much. She'd head straight for the forest. Straight for the grave that she still believed I was lying and buried within. And when she didn't find me there…then what? She'd finally come home, back to this humble adobe, that's what. She'd want to find dad and find out from the horse's mouth what he'd done with me. Where I'd gone? And why he had dug me up and taken me away.

What would happen that, I couldn't be so sure.

Perhaps this place was to be my new home from now on. Down here in the dark. My sister would go about her daily life in the house above while I rotted away down here like a wee, starving, dirty rat.

Would my sister really let that happen though? Would she?

I had to believe that the answer to that was no. I had to. I just had to. With all my heart and all of my soul, I had to hope that she would come and save me, somehow. Surely, she would find a way.

As the day limped on, my eyes began to adjust more to the darkness and I found myself just about seeing from one end of the cellar room I had called my own all the way through to the next doorway.

The ground beneath my feet was solid concrete, but the edges of the cellar walls were a mixture of stone and dirt, and I eventually found some worms in amongst the mix. Begrudgingly, I ate them. I ate them all. I found some beetles too and then a few large spiders in some of the darkest and dampest corners of the rooms. I'd seen my sister on countless occasions finding then eating spiders. She'd always enjoyed slowly ripping their legs apart from their bulging fat bodies, one my one, before shoving them into her mouth and chewing them up like they were tastier than a pack of chocolate buttons.

I always swore that I'd never do such a thing like eating a spider. Ever. Not even if my life depended on it. It was disgusting and made my skin absolutely shiver and crawl. But desperate times called for desperate measures. I wasn't too sure if my life depended on it just yet, but here I found myself nonetheless.

So, I didn't even think about it. I just grabbed its darting, creepy little body, as quickly as I could, clutching it hard in my hands. I shoved the wee buggers into my mouth whole, without even a second thought, twitching legs and all.

I must have eaten about ten of the horrid wee creatures in total by the time evening came around and I heard my father's car pull up in front of the house. When he stepped out of the car and walked towards the front door, my little heart sank to the pit of my stomach.

I knew it was him but I wished upon a thousand falling stars that it would have been my sister. I soon heard him cooking in the kitchen, then singing along to the radio. I tried to cover my ears but it didn't do any good. I could still hear his horrendous and vile sounds, and my hatred for him was boiling and bubbling into overdrive.

I listened as he ate his meal in the living room before returning to the kitchen to wash his dishes. When he was done cleaning up, I heard him move faintly up to the first floor of the house. After that he went silent for a very long time.

Chapter 19

Deep into the night, as I was just about to drift off up against the most comfortable bit of stone dirt wall I could find, I heard someone's frantic footsteps running up towards the farmhouse. At first, I thought I was dreaming. Immediately, my ears pricked up and I sat upright, alert and stiff. I heard the front door swing open, followed by more frantic footsteps on the creaking wooden floors above.

In a heartbeat I knew it was her. My sister had returned and it had only been around two or three full days, I think.

I felt so overjoyed and with what little strength I had left in my body I jumped immediately onto my feet. I wanted to shout out to her that I was all right, that I was down in the cellar. I wanted to cry out her name so, so much but at the same time I swiftly restrained myself from doing so. My father was still upstairs. If he heard me, then I truly believed there was no telling what he might do to me or to her.

I heard my sister approach the main stairs leading up to the first floor of the house. I heard her call out my father's name. A long silent pause filled the air. At the second time of calling out for him, I finally heard him shouting back at her from the top of the upstairs landing. He seemed to be in relatively good spirits. Chuffed to bits that she'd made it all the way back to our home in such a short space of time.

I heard my sister cutting him off, though, which was uncharacteristic for her, and swiftly asking about me. He probably wouldn't have liked that very much. In my mind's eye, I could see his smug smile turning into a miserable frown. Before he could even answer, I heard my sister say to him that she'd been to the woods already. That she'd seen the dug-up, empty grave. She wanted to know what he'd done to me. She wanted to know if I was still alive.

He told her to calm the hell down. He told her that I was safe and sound. That she would see me soon enough. Sooner than she thought, in fact. When she demanded to know exactly where I was, he coolly and calmly stated that he had me locked away down in the basement for safe keeping until she'd returned. I felt surprised that he'd made that admission so open and freely. It made me even more cautious and suspicious of his intentions regarding both our wellbeing. It made me wonder what cruel and twisted game he was going to play next with us. I honestly didn't have a clue. I was at a stalemate.

I heard my dad slowly dismount the main stairs of the house. He told my sister that she should go to the kitchen and have something to eat. That he'd cooked a meal for both of us earlier and that she should take it down to the basement and eat it with me.

I held my breath as I heard them enter the kitchen. I heard the plates being shoved into the microwave. I heard the microwave being turned on, full power, for a long time. I heard my sister and dad talking more but, because of the microwave's constant humming, I couldn't hear a damn word of what they were saying. I heard my father raise his voice a few times, but still I couldn't hear what was being discussed.

Someone finally took the plates out of the microwave oven. I think it was dad who grabbed them and handed them over to my sister. I heard their footsteps moving towards the hidden cellar entrance. I followed their sound until I reached the locked iron door in the middle of the dark basement.

I heard their footsteps coming down the narrow staircase. Coming down towards me. I heard the squeaky, rusty bolts being pulled back on the door. Then the huge iron key in the lock. I took a few steps back. The door creaked open. I hid behind the open doorway of the room I was standing in, directly opposite the iron door. I held my breath again as I peeked through the darkness. My sister's shadow stepped inside. The dim light from the staircase beyond her was like a brief sunrise in the basement darkness. It lit up almost every nook and cranny in its path. Then the door was swiftly sealed and bolted shut again. The darkness returned as the sound of father's footsteps mounted the stairs, back up towards the main house.

I stepped out from the doorway. I saw my sister standing in front of the iron door, holding two plates of potatoes and beef stew. She turned in my direction when she heard my movements, but she couldn't see me just yet. Her eyes hadn't fully adjusted to the pitch-black cellar darkness like my eyes had.

Suddenly, she spoke.

"Are ye there, sister?"

I took a long time to answer. I was so happy just to see her voice. I felt over the moon just to hear her stiff voice one more time. I imagined hugging her hard, then crying and sobbing into each other's arms. But by the way we'd been brought up over the years—to show no emotion, no empathy, even towards the ones closest to us—I knew my sister would be reluctant to make such an emotional reunion.

"I'm here," I finally said, edging a few more steps closer to her.

"Here. Take the plate. It's fur you," she said so causal, like she'd never been away and had been down in that dark, grimy cellar with me the whole time.

I did as she asked and took the plate from her hands.

"Can ye take mines tae?" she asked. "Ah have a lighter and a candle in ma pocket. A bottle of water tae. If ye hold ma plate ah can get them."

I did as she asked and held her plate with my other hand.

I watched as she pulled out a candle and a lighter from one of her jacket pockets. Only it wasn't her jacket at all. It was new. She hadn't been wearing it the last time I saw her while digging my grave.

"Nice jacket," I casually stated as she sparked the lighter three times before finally being able to light the candle.

"Ah stole it yesterday. On the way back doon fae the Island."

"You were fast," I replied. The candle lit up the surrounding basement corridor. With the new light, we both paused for a few moments and stared at each other, deep into one another's eyes. From the neck up, even though she was a wee bit taller, it was like glancing into a mirror. Her face looked so dirty. Probably just as dirty as mine. Eventually, we both smiled warmly.

"Your face is so dirty," I pointed out.

"Ah was thinking the same thing aboot you."

We both smiled at that.

"Come on then, sister," she said, before walking past me and stepping into the room that I was standing in the doorway of. "Let's sit doon and eat. Am hungry as fuck and am sure we have a lot of things tae chat aboot."

I'd forgotten how alike she was with our father. Not just by the way she acted, but by the way she sounded too. From her aggressive and alpha body language to the way she spoke without fear. Like every word she spoke had some kind of meaning or importance.

I followed her with the plates of stew. We sat down opposite each other in the middle of the cold, hard room. My sister pulled out a bottle of water from her other pocket and left it standing between our seated bodies. She pulled out two forks and handed me one. I thanked her and took mine. Then I began to eat. My sister started eating too, fork in one hand, lighted candle in the other.

"How did you make it back here so fast?" I asked between spoonful's of stew that I couldn't shove into my mouth quick enough. I was so damn hungry.

"Ah jist snuck back on board that ferry again," she said like it had been no hassle at all. And it probably wasn't. "Aye, it wis pretty easy. Once ah reached the mainland ah walked fur a wee bit. Then ah stole a car fae some family of dozy tourists who were huvin a wee picnic nearby."

"Jesus Christ," I uttered. Shocked that she went against my father's wishes and did something so bold and illegal like that, which would not just bring attention to her but to us, to our own father even. "I thought dad said not to do anything like that. Nothing to draw attention. Keep your head down."

"Fuck him!" she said with a mischievous grin. I felt genuinely shocked by her statement. "Ah had to get back hame tae ma sister. And besides, if he didnae want us drawing any attention tae him or oorselves then he shouldnae have dumped us in the middle of fuckin naewhere and asked us tae find oor own way hame again."

I gently shook my head and continued to eat. I'd never heard my sister talk like that about dad before. To talk down on him. To criticise him. She seemed genuinely pissed with him too. Was she now suddenly beginning to see the light also? Was she finally seeing my father in the way in which I saw him? An absolute bloody sadistic lunatic who shouldn't be allowed on the same planet as children, let alone be able to parent them.

There were no further words spoken between my sister and I for quite some time. Well, not until we'd both finished our meals, wiped our mouths, and drank some water. My sister then pulled out her huge hunting knife that was strapped onto her belt at the back of her trousers. She placed the knife gently down on the hard-concrete floor. I didn't fully understand why she had done it at first. I thought that it might just be uncomfortable for her to have it tucked into her belt while she sat and ate.

"You huv tae kill me sister?" she suddenly said, flat and with no emotion and completely out of the blue. I felt totally taken back. Utterly shocked. I couldn't believe what she'd just said. I felt extremely rocked to my core by her bizarre, random, and matter-of-fact statement. Had I misheard her?

"What… what are you talking about?" I finally stuttered.

"Dad says that anly wan of us can leave this place noo. He wants either me tae kill you or you tae kill me. He said he anly wants the strongest of us to walk oot of here alive."

Again, I was totally lost for words. Struck dumb with disbelief.

"What… what the hell are you talking about? We can't kill each other. That's absurd!"

"He expects it tae be me tae walk oot of this cellar alive, sis, and your dead body tae be left tae rot doon here with the dust, dirt, the creepy crawlies… even oor ain mother. He knows, in fact, he's convinced, that when it comes doon tae it, ah will go through with whatever he asks of me noo."

Tears began rolling down my cheeks like little crystal snow balls. I couldn't stop them. They were a mix of anger and sorrow. Was this some kind of sick and twisted joke? How could she say such a thing, and say it too with such calm and total lack of emotion?

"So why are you still talking to me then, huh?" I cried, getting angrier, getting upset. "Why haven't you killed me already if you're so cold, heartless, and callous just like him?"

My sister took a long, deep, and very hard breath. After a long, excruciatingly strung-out moment, she finally glanced away from me and sighed.

"Cuz ah think, in ma heart, ah dinnae want tae be like him anymare, sis. Ah think, deep doon inside, ah always wanted tae be like you. Ah always wanted tae be brave and strong just like you. Ah wanted tae be good and liked, just like you were when we were baeth at school. Dae you remember?"

"But you are brave and strong!" I protested. "You are, sister. *You are.* So much, much more than me. So much more."

My sister lightly shook her head.

"No, yur the brave one. Yur the strong one. Yur the one who wullnae change for him. Yur the one who fights what he wants us tae become. Yur the one who doesnae want tae follow him or listen tae his words. Who wants tae escape fae this life? Who dreams of something better? Do ye no see, sister? You are the strong and brave one here. Everything yuv said tae defy him, maybe no oot loud, but av heard yur thoughts. Av seen your true feelings in yur eyes and in yur face and in yur entire body, every time yur aroond him."

"Aw av ever done is been his sheep. His wee fuckin lamb. Ah follow his every word. Everything he's ever asked of me av done or become tae one extent or another. Ah just wanted him tae like me at the heart of it, that's aw. Even tae love me. Ah just wanted someone tae like me or love me for who ah am, ye know. And no huvin tae dae aw these stupid tests and games to prove masel aw the time."

"But I love you, sister," I blurted out through my tears, interrupting her. "I love you more than anything or anyone else in this world."

"Ah just wanted tae make him prood," my sister continued, not really listening to me anymore. "But whit he does, whit he makes us dae, whit he's aw aboot, it's none of that stuff. And al never get the things ah truly yearn fae him, fae a father, ever. Ah realise that noo. Ah think av always known it, secretly, deep doon. But ah anly ever truly realised it when he made me bury you in that grave oot there in they woods. And noo... noo ah think he's realised that tae. Why else did he take ye fae they woods and put you doon here? He knew, that if ah would have went straight back tae they woods, dug you up, and foond ye alive, then he'd never see or hear fae either of us again. We'd run like the wind and disappear intae the distant horizon like two migrating birds."

"But, you, sister..." she went on. "Yuv always known what he is. Always, but still ye defy him. Even noo. That's real strength, sister. That's true bravery and character. Knowing what he's capable of. Aw those mad horrible things he's done, yet still you defy him. And ah think that terrifies the life oot of him more than anything else in the world. Knowing that whitever he says tae you, whitever he does, he can never, ever change ye. He can never change ye tae his way of thinking like he's done tae me."

I didn't know what to say. I didn't know what to do. My tears had blinded me and my internal sobs had rendered me speechless.

My sister picked up her knife and handed it over to me. As soon as the handle touched my fingers, I immediately jerked my hands away and placed them securely behind my back. Not a chance on god's green earth would I ever take that knife from her grasp. Not a chance.

"No," I sobbed. "No! No way will I do such a thing. I will not lay one finger on you. I will never lay a finger on you even if he comes down here and tortures me to death this very instant, I will still never lay a finger of harm on you. I love you, sis. I love you."

In the flicker of the candle light, I watched as my sister just grinned again and gently shook her head.

"Ah thought ye might say sumhing silly like that and prove ma point. So, we'll baeth rot and starve doon here then, aye? And what good will that dae either of us, eh sister?"

I shook my head. I knew I wouldn't let that happen either. If only one of us was getting out of here alive, then by any power and strength remaining inside me, it would be my sister. No doubt about it.

I glanced at the knife. I knew then what I needed to do. I went to make a swift grab for it, but my sister had already read my mind long before the actions of my body took over and did my mind's bidding.

My sister swiftly pulled the knife away. She turned the blade towards her, lifted her arms up as far back as they would go. She looked me dead in the eye before smiling warmly for the first time that I could ever remember. Before I could even gasp or put together another thought, my sister plunged the knife deep and hard, right into the gut of her belly.

She let out a loud gasp and a hideous, hideous winded yelp.

Before I could react, before I could even do or say anything, she shocked and tortured me further by ripping the knife right back out of her belly and, in the blink of an eye, raising it up to her neck and slashing her own throat from left to right.

The blood poured out of her. Both wounds ran like a river of red. I really thought I was dreaming or hallucinating again. Surely, this wasn't real. It was only a dream. It was only a dream.

My sister fell back onto the cold hard floor, face up and staring blankly into the flickering candle-light shadows of dark and light above as the life drained swiftly out of her. Just like when I'd watched the life drain out of Chris only a few days earlier.

She coughed and spluttered. She started gasping and wheezing for breath. The paralysing horror of the moment finally lifted its heavy hands from upon my shoulders and my body unfroze. I jumped to her side. I lifted her head and cradled her in my arms.

"Why...?" I sobbed. "Why did you do that? Why?"

She tried to speak while spitting up more blood.

"If ye want... tae get oot of here sis... tae be truly free fae him..." she tried to utter in between gasps and wheezes of blood and air. "...then in his eyes... you huv tae be me... ye huv tae be me for at least a little while, sister, in order tae dae that..."

I continued to shake my head. I sobbed even harder.

"No, no, no..." I cried over and over. I couldn't believe that my sister was dying, right in front of my very eyes. It wasn't real. It wasn't real, I kept telling myself. Any minute now she was going to dig me up from that grave out in the woods, wake me up from the nightmares and shadows and drag me back up into the world of the living, kicking and screaming. A world where we could live well and die free together, run wild together, just *be together.*

My sister held out her limp, bloodied hand. I took it instantly, sandwiching it between both of my own. I watched as her breathing became shallower. I watched and cried as the life force drained out of her beautiful, pale wee face.

I watched as she died in my arms.

I watched my own death.

My brave, strong, beautiful sister gone from this world.

Taken, but not taken by her own hand. No, I'd never admit to something like that, not ever. Yes, she was taken from me. But taken from me by another's guilty hand. Another still living and walking and breathing in this world.

Chapter 20

When dad woke up early the next morning the first thing he did was come all the way down to the cellar and call out from behind the locked iron door.

"Is it done?" he cried before banging furiously upon the door half a dozen times. "Is it done, ah said?"

In the darkness of the cellar, I sat beside my dead sister. She looked so pale. She felt so cold and hard lying in my arms. So unnatural in her dead shell. I still held her hand tightly too, like I had done so throughout the entire night, only letting it go once to change out of my clothes and carefully dressing into hers just like she'd asked me to. Just like she wanted me too, even though I still had her dried blood all over me.

"Dinnae make me open this fuckin door and come in there noo!" dad continued to rant and rave and bang even harder. "Answer me! Someone. For fuck's sake. If it's no done, then it'll be a week before ah come back again. Then a month after that. Ye can baeth fuckin starve in there for aw ah care!"

I took a deep breath and finally let go of my sister. I stood gently up and casually walked over towards the door. I knocked hard from my side and said to dad that it was done in the most unemotional and uncaring voice I could muster, a tone that resembled my sister's.

My father opened the iron door. He wore a big, beaming grin all over his face. He strolled right on past me and straight into the room where my dead and bloodied sister laid—where *I* still laid.

He crouched down to touch her. He even took her pulse, like that was really necessary. He turned back towards me.

"Ye did good, girl. Ye did fuckin good!"

He stood up and walked back towards me.

"Noo. Ah need ye tae dae one mare hing, and then… and then ye really will be yur faither's girl."

Dad slapped me on the shoulder and motioned me out of the dark cellar. For a second, I was about to turn around and ask him about my sister's body. Were we really just going to leave her down there, like she was nothing, nothing but a dead rodent? I almost asked too. But then I remembered who I was supposed to be so I didn't say a word. I just bit my tongue and walked up those lonely, steep, narrow steps towards the ground floor of the house without looking back.

   ***

I was in the car again and dad was driving. Driving his car and playing his tunes and singing along like he always did whilst driving. Acting like he didn't have a care in the world. Which he sadly did not.

We were heading down towards Glasgow again. Heading out for another adventure. Another of his games that he wanted to play. And without my sister dragging me back, his words. He was convinced that I would now follow through, without hesitation, any challenge that he put down in front of me.

Since it was just the two of us, he wanted me to sit up front with him. So, I did with no questions asked. I just sat in silence. With my head always turned and glancing out the window at the passing mountains, towns, valleys, and lochs. I tried my best to zone out of anything he was doing or saying. Even when he tried to get a wee bit of rapport going between us by telling me one of his own sick and twisted confessions.

"Ye ken, ah had a brother once tae when ah was your age."

This was the first time I'd ever heard him speak about anyone from his family before who wasn't his own father.

"And ma faither made me dae exactly what ah just made ye dae, doon there in that cellar. We werenae twins like you and that…" he hesitated. Like he couldn't even say her name, *my* name, anymore. "… like ye and that other lass. He was ma older brother by a year. And ah fucking killed the cunt when the time came. Nay hesitation. Just boom! Knife straight tae the belly. Anly the strongest survive in this world, ma girl. Anly the strongest."

He sounded so smug and proud while making that statement, like it was the only thing left to say that would cement our bond and connection, sealing it together once and for all.

"Yur strong, ma girl. Strong like me. And when it comes, when the shit truly hits the fan one day very soon, when that fuckin sky opens and swallows up aw the shite and scum of this world—chews them aw up and spits them aw oot—well, yull thank me for this one day. Yul thank me for every wee hing av ever taught ye, lass. Ah promise ye that, ma girl. Ah promise ye that much."

He tried to give me a wee half hug but nearly steered the car off the road in the process. I zoned him out as best as I could after that. I just wanted him to stop talking and start singing again. Anything but to have to sit and listen to him talk about his end-of-the-world garbage.

I grabbed the handle of my sister's knife tucked snuggly away inside the deep pockets of her jacket. I squeezed that handle so hard and so tight for such a long time. But that's all I did for the time being. I wasn't as brave and as strong as my sister to take that next final step just yet and put that knife somewhere, someplace where the sun didn't shine.

When I released my hold on the knife again, I got the strangest feeling in the pit of my tummy. I felt another presence inside the car. I half turned to the seat behind only to see my sister sitting in the back and staring right at me. She looked so lifelike and real. Like she hadn't died at all. She gave me a warm, reassuring smile. She looked so pretty and radiant and so at peace with the world. I'd never seen her like that before. I smiled back at her. She then motioned for me to put the seat down and my head right back, which I did.

"Aye, better get some rest, ma girl. Yuv goat a long night ahead of ye yet," dad said when he saw me pushing my seat down as far as it would go into the back of the car.

My sister then took my hair and began to massage her fingers all around my scalp. It felt so good. So relaxing and soothing. It was like all my worries and stress just melted away in that moment. I knew then that as long as I could see my sister, feel her, or speak to her whenever I wanted to, then everything would be all right. When I finally closed my eyes and gave myself into the massage, I quickly fell into a deep and blissful sleep.

***

It was late, around midnight I think, when we finally drove into Glasgow city centre. Dad shook me awake and said we were there. As I pushed my seat back up into its proper position, I made a swift glance into the back seat but my sister wasn't anywhere to be seen.

My hair felt strange though, tight and firm. When I touched it with my hands, I discovered that she'd braided it into a ponytail while I'd slept. I'd never had my hair in a pony tail before. Especially a braided one. I had a long look in the reflection of the car window. I really liked it. And if my sister wanted me to have one, then I'd keep it.

Dad parked outside a big McDonald's and lead me inside. He said I could have whatever I liked from the menu. I didn't feel like eating anything though. I wasn't hungry in the slightest, but I had to order something. Just to go along with the act. Just to show him that everything was still the same.

Dad ordered and paid for the meals. We sat at a window seat and ate them together in silence. I noticed a lot of sad-looking people in that place. No one talked. They just sat and ate with their heads bowed down and faces buried into their phones. I glanced out of the window instead and watched the rain. It was in between light and heavy, but strangely jagged and slashing down in a diagonal wave which made it look as if it were pouring down from the high, city centre rooftops rather than the grey heavens above. I liked the rain. It felt strangely hypnotic and reminded me of the rare, quieter and peaceful times in the company of my sister, both of us sitting comfortably by ourselves on the livingroom couch of our remote highland home, reading our books while the shower of rain outside pitter pattered off the windows.

When we were finished with our meals we got back into the car and drove around some of the quiet back streets of the city for a while. I knew what dad was looking for now. And I knew what he wanted me to do in order to prove myself to him, one last time.

When he gently pulled up outside a dark alleyway, where a drunken, old homeless man—maybe in his fifties—was struggling to pull up his trousers, I knew dad had found his final piece in his perfect, little picture of his father-and-daughter jigsaw.

He turned off the engine.

"Mon you. Get oot."

He got out of the car and I slowly followed after him. The homeless man was still trying to pull up his trousers but he just couldn't seem to pull them up properly. It was like his entire upper body was working in slow motion as he tried desperately to reach down and at least grab his belt. No matter how hard he tried, though, he just couldn't seem to get a good enough hold of them to pull them up. I had no idea why his trousers and pants were down around his ankles, in the first place. I didn't want to know.

Dad approached the homeless man from behind and grabbed him by the scruff of his neck.

"Right you, ye cunt."

He dragged the homeless man into the alleyway. He dragged him over bins and bags of old rubbish before throwing him hard against the back-brick wall. The homeless man slid fast down the wall and onto his backside. He looked so wasted. He didn't seem to have a clue in holy hell what was happening. He looked long gone from this world. A picture of the walking dead. Surprisingly though he started to laugh. Then when dad pulled out his big hunting knife, he began to cry instead.

I moved a wee bit closer towards the pair. Dad was leaning into the man, now, as he sat and cried. I knew what dad intended for me to do without even being asked. I knew in my gut what he'd wanted from me. And if I didn't act fast and did what he asked, then I'd surely be found out. I'd no doubt end up like my sister. Or that woman he tried to make us kill. Or that camper in the woods. Or Chris. Or this sorry and sad looking homeless man who was about to meet his maker.

Without even thinking about it, I pulled out my sister's hunting knife from my jacket pocket.

"Whit a fuckin sad, pathetic piece of shite," dad said to the homeless man. "Fuckin scumbag junkie fuckheed if ah ever saw yin."

I stood in silence beside my dad.

"Hoo the fuck are ye even still alive, ye fuckin useless cunt ye? Ah mean, whit fuckin use are ye tae any cunt in this world, eh? Whit fuckin use are ye son? Ye fuckin useless sack of shite."

"Am sorry," the man continued sobbing.

Up close and behind his scruffy and scraggily beard, filthy ripped jeans, shirt, and jacket he looked more like mid-thirties now rather than fifty. For one moment I began thinking deeply about how a person could end up like this. What horrific things or string of bad luck did a person have to go through in order to live out on the street like this. Bur before I could think too much, his pleading and sobs brought me back to reality again.

"Ah didnae mean it. Ah anly wanted tae go tae ma bed. Am sorry man. Am really sorry. Ah didnae know this wiz yur bit, pal. Yur alleyway, ma man. Ah didnae know. Ah jist wanted ma bed. Ah jist wanted tae go tae ma bed."

"Go tae yur bed, ye cunt?" dad shot back. "Al put ye tae yur fuckin bed, awright, ye fuckin jakey cunt! Ye fuckin plague tae society. Al fuckin put ye tae sleep, awright!"

Out of the darkness, my sister silently stepped up beside me. She put her hand gently upon my shoulder. I turned to face her. When I looked at her she just smiled warmly and nodded at me like she knew exactly what I was thinking. Like she knew what needed to be done here. It had to be done.

She took a hold of my knife hand and guided it in the direction it needed to go.

"We're gonna play a wee fuckin game, you and I, son," dad continued to rant and rave. "It's cawed 'hide the fuckin blade.'"

Dad unleashed a devilish grin. He started to turn his face towards mine. His eyes were on fire, blazing from the pupils within with an insane rage and desire. I'd seen pictures of various interpretations of the devil before, but they were nothing like this. Nothing like him.

"You are ready," he said to me. "You are fuckin ready, ma girl!" dad roared.

He was just about to give me the nod. His blessing to step up to the homeless man and do my thing. To bury my knife anywhere on his body that took my fancy and bury it deeply and repetitively at that.

Dad was right. We were ready.

As dad locked his eyes into mine and gave out that familiar, sadistic, sinister, old grin of his, not a second sooner nor without any further hesitation, did we both then drive that large hunting knife home together.

My sister and I.

Together as one.

We plunged that long, thick, sharp blade deep and hard, right up to the hilt of the handle, all the way in and through and finally to the back of my father's vein-bulging throat.

I think, in that moment, he caught a quick glimpse of the two of us together again, side by side. One last time. His two, brave, little daughters.

The way his eyes darted from one of us to the other in those last few moments—from my sister to me, then back to my sister again, still standing, cold, stern, and hard beside me—he must have known.

As the blood began to spray then slowly ooze out of him like the red Falls of Clyde, he finally dropped his knife to the ground. He raised his hands, meekly up towards his throat. He desperately tried to clutch the knife handle and pull it out from his severed wind pipe but, alas, he couldn't do it. The strength and life were draining from him thick and fast, and the knife, as far as I could tell, had wedged itself into the roof of his spine and the back bones of his neck.

He let go of the handle and staggered back. I thought he might fall backwards with an almighty thud, but then he surprised me by falling down onto his knees instead.

He glanced up at both me and my sister again. Neither of us had moved. We both remained callously still. Neither one of us had uttered a word or even took a breath for that matter. None of us were showing any emotion or remorse at the brutal and violent act we had just participated in and committed together.

I swear he almost looked proud. After what seemed like an eternity, but was probably no more than a minute or so, dad fell flat on his face and died.

After a short while, I turned fully around to face my sister again. My sister turned to face me. We looked at each other long and hard. We both knew instantly what the other was thinking.

So, this was what freedom looked like.

So, this was what freedom tasted like.

This was how it felt to be *free*.

I hugged my sister as hard as I possibly could for the very first time in my life and she, in turn, hugged me too.

Before we left the alley, I went through my father's pockets. I took his wallet and car keys. When my sister and I finally left the alleyway together, hand in hand, the homeless man was lying flat on his back, passed out on his drugs and booze, and snoring for Scotland like nothing had ever happened. He would wake up later, believing everything that had happened to him in the alleyway to be nothing more than a dream. Well, until he saw my father's dead body lying there beside him.

We didn't care though. We didn't give a holy damned hell. My sister and I were free to do what we liked. And there was a whole, wide, new world out there for us to explore. Although there was one more thing I wanted to do first before I embarked on this new adventure of our life together. I wanted to drive all the way back up to our house again. I wanted to climb back down into that cellar. I wanted to take both my sister's and my mother's remains out of that disgusting hell-hole and give them the proper burial they deserved. Out in the open somewhere, some place in nature more fitting for them than the insides of some cold, dark and miserable cellar. Maybe on the edge of the forest, close to a loch or on one of the clifftops near our home.

I climbed into dad's car and made myself comfortable in the passenger's seat. My sister climbed into the driver's side and took a firm hold of the wheel. Out of the two of us, she was the one who could drive. She was the one who was better at finding her way home than me. She would have us both back in no time at all.

She allowed me to be in charge of the radio though. That was my job for this journey. Passenger DJ. And as I found a nice, soft rock tune on the radio to get our road trip back up to the highlands started, my sister put the key into the ignition, started the engine, slid the car into gear, and drove us home.

The End

Thank you for purchasing my Novel 'My Sister and I'

If you enjoyed this novel and would like to help, then you could think about leaving a review on Amazon, Goodreads or anywhere else that readers visit. The most important part of how well a book sells is how many positive reviews it has, so if you leave me one, then you are directly helping me to continue on this journey as a fulltime writer.

A huge big thank you in advance to anyone who does.

It means a lot.

Cheers and many thanks for your time and interest in my self-published books.

You can read more of my work here:

www.amazon.com/Sean-Paul-Thomas/

www.amazon.co.uk/Wrath-David-Sean-Paul-Thomas-

www.goodreads.com/book/show/36436831-the-wrath-of-david

You can connect with me here:

https://www.facebook.com/SeanPaulThomasAuthor

mailto:seanpaulthomasauthor@aol.com

36508083R00095

Printed in Great Britain
by Amazon